Capturi

The K

Samai

Edited by Dom's Proofreading
Proofed by Destini Reece and Em Petrova
Cover art by Midnight Muse Designs

Chapter One

A silent scream built inside Grace.

She clasped her hands tightly together and glanced down at her blanching knuckles. Her heart throbbed hard in her chest. One more month and she would be independent.

No. She *would* have been independent.

And she would have taken her inheritance, whisked her aunt away from the vile man that was her husband, and they could have lived in peace for the rest of their days.

Now she had mere days before that dream was shattered.

She glanced down at where her fingers pinched into the backs of her hands and she spied little red marks forming around each fingertip, yet she could not release them, or she might really scream.

What would happen if she unleashed it upon the man who had been her guardian for so many years? Would he even notice her? Uncle Charlie had always done his best to avoid her, even when she had arrived here, an orphaned child of just eight years old. Had it not been for her wonderful aunt—her father's sister—life would have been miserable indeed.

Of course, once the terms of her inheritance had been revealed, he'd paid a little more attention. Grace knew exactly why her uncle was trying to marry her off before her twenty-first birthday.

Especially to a man like Mr. Worthington.

She snorted to herself. Worthy, he was not. In fact, he was downright terrifying.

Shooting her gaze from man to man, she could not see a single positive trait in either of them whilst they discussed Grace's future as though she were not even in the room.

Uncle Charlie had always suffered a sallow complexion, with deep hollowed eyes. His cold gaze never warmed, not even upon viewing his wife or something that would thaw the heart of the coldest man. No kittens or children playing, or beautiful sunsets could reach his frozen heart as far as she was concerned.

It was likely shielded behind a thick wall of greed, built from the coin he scrabbled for then spent so frivolously. Her poor aunt had been forced to make excuses for many a debt and sell off most of her jewelry and fine clothing.

Meanwhile, Uncle Charlie dressed as finely as ever, only wearing the best fabrics and latest fashions.

Grace wrinkled her nose. Not that it helped him as he aged. His hair had thinned at a rapid rate, leaving a few thick, dark strands clinging to the shiny dome of his head, and a strip of shorter hair curving around the back of his head. He was growing smaller too but still stood tall over Grace which frustrated her to no end. How she wished she could rise from this chair, look down her nose at him, and tell him in no uncertain terms that she refused to marry Mr. Worthington.

She tried to eye him dispassionately, and not through the veil of fear that seeped inside her every time he stepped in the room but failed. She loathed to be one to fall for rumors but as soon as she met Mr. Worthington, she knew them to be true.

If her uncle's eyes appeared cold, Mr. Worthington's pale blue ones were downright ice. Combined with that constant curve at the corners of his lips that told her here was a man who was used to getting everything he wanted in life—whether it via force or coercion—the man who was to be her husband left her more than empty inside.

While she had never enjoyed sweeping dreams of love as some girls did, she certainly didn't imagine marrying a man twenty years her senior who had only recently buried his wife after she had been found sprawled at the bottom of the stairs.

And everyone knew why.

Good God, she couldn't marry the man. But what could she do? Even if she did rise from her seat, and try to scream as loud as she could, her uncle was her guardian until her twenty-first birthday. It was impossible to defy him. If only she could get him to delay the marriage somehow. Or she could run away and hide for a while. But how? And where? She didn't even like visiting new houses let alone dashing off to goodness knows where—alone—and hoping she did not get hurt.

Which was highly likely.

Not only was she ignorant to the world, she was small—too small. Her tiny frame and small stature had always made her vulnerable.

How she loathed it. If only she were tall and commanding and able to tell her uncle in no uncertain terms that she would not marry a man like Mr. Worthington—or any man for that matter—and she would be taking her father's money thank you very much, and moving somewhere peaceful and quiet, and surrounding herself with all the things she loved.

Mr. Worthington glanced her way. Only briefly, mind, as though she were of no consequence. As though their discussion of her wedding day had nothing to do with her. Of course, it was mostly to do with her inheritance, so she supposed it did not really. The fact he had to take her as his wife meant little if he could lay claim to her money.

Grace lifted her gaze to the ceiling, eyeing the grand, plaster rose that circled a small chandelier. Why could her father not have willed the money directly to her? Why did he think she might wish to marry? Surly he knew his eloquent, bookish daughter would never want a man?

She sighed. Her father had been trying to look after her with his terms, she knew that. By ensuring her money would go to her husband upon her marriage, regardless of her age, he was making sure she was an attractive prospect and that no financial worries would put off a potential suitor.

He did not, however, expect her uncle to make some sordid deal with a man like Worthington, just so he could take a share of said money once it was in her husband's hands.

The scream began building again, filling her lungs and making her throat hot. Except she knew if she even tried to unleash it, it would come out as a mere squeak, just like when Freddy Porter pinned her against the church door and kissed her or when Eliza McConnell made fun of her lack of curves when all the other girls were growing into women.

She'd tried to scream and shout and stamp her feet but there was nothing intimidating or scary about a slight woman like her throwing a strop and they simply laughed at her.

Mr. Worthington caught her eye and the corners of his lips fell back into a smug smirk. Though he was not ugly for his age, she saw straight through his thick, gray-black hair, strong jaw, and refined nose.

She saw straight to the core of him, even if he tried to keep it hidden—which he had initially when he'd made noises about courting her. She ignored him. Her inheritance was not public knowledge, for which she was grateful. Otherwise she might have been forced to ignore more suitors. But her quiet temperament and scrawny body kept them at bay regardless.

Until horrible, horrible Mr. Worthington.

Oh, he'd tried to charm her. Tried to flatter her vanity. Well, more fool him. She had no vanity. She might have had the odd pang of envy at Eliza McConnell's curves, but her father had taught her better than that. A woman should be more than the sum of her looks.

Thus, Mr. Worthington found his overtures flatly ignored. Why should she give up her hope of independence for a flirtatious smile and a few flattering words? No, she was determined she would never marry and certainly never hand over her father's hard-earned fortune to her husband.

If only her uncle felt the same.

Mr. Worthington rose, and Grace realized they'd finished their discussion of her and the plans for their wedding. Just the thought made her want to vomit right here, in front of Mr. Worthington. If she did so, would he run away scared perhaps? She glanced up at him as she rose from her seat. No, he'd take her, vomit and all, just for her fortune, and then she would be trapped in an awful situation like his last wife.

How long would it be until she was a pile of broken bones at the bottom of the stairs?

God, she had to escape somehow.

"Well, I shall call upon you again next week." Mr. Worthington took her hand and brushed a kiss across her knuckles. She flinched but he kept her hand held firm while her stomach hurt so much, she wanted to fold in two. His grin widened at her reaction. "I cannot wait to make you my wife," he murmured.

Grace didn't reply. What could she say? *I'd rather die first?*

Perhaps, but she would far rather survive and make her father proud. If only there were some easy way to escape, some forgotten cousin somewhere who would give her shelter. But it was only her and her aunt and how could she leave Aunt Elsie alone with awful Uncle Charlie? He'd no doubt blame her for Grace's disappearance and, though he was not inclined to use his fists like everyone said Mr. Worthington did, he could make her miserable enough.

Her uncle closed the door behind Mr. Worthington and folded his arms across a broad, slightly rotund chest. "You would do well to be pleasant to him, Grace. He will make you a fine husband."

"How so, Uncle?"

"He's attractive, well-connected..." His brow furrowed. "For God's sakes, girl. This is the first offer you've had. You should be grateful."

It was so tempting to unleash that scream now. Or shout at him. Tell him she knew he was selling her off. But her fate was in his hands. Perhaps if she was polite...

"Please do not make me marry him," she begged, disliking how strangled her voice was. It only made her more vulnerable. Lord, how she hated it. "He shall hurt me, you know he shall," she added when his expression remained unchanged.

He waved a hand. "He will do no such thing." A finger thrust toward her and she stared at the slightly ink-stained tip as it wavered in front of her. "Whoever put about those rumors was simply trying to hurt Mr. Worthington's fine reputation. I have only ever found him to be the most pleasing of men. Besides, why would a good-looking, charming chap like Worthington need to hurt a woman? No doubt he gave his wife a good spanking every now and then but what woman hasn't needed a spanking?"

She hadn't. Her father would never do such a thing, nor would he have done it to her mother, she knew that much. He spoke many times of the mutual respect they had for one another and the importance of proper discourse when one disagreed with the other. But there would be no proper discourse with her uncle, of that she was certain.

"You would sell me off, Uncle, regardless," she muttered.

"Pardon?" he barked.

She shook her head and eyed the blood red carpet, weaved with gold and green patterns. How she hated this carpet. Hated this room with all its masculine overtones of dark mahogany and flecks of gold. She preferred her aunt's threadbare parlor with its soft, pale laces and plump cushions and pretty sceneries thrifted from goodness knows where.

How she hated that her uncle sat in luxury every day while his wife was neglected and left with nothing and she tried to pay off the debts her uncle constantly accrued. All the best jewelry and gowns were gone, all the family heirlooms. All so her uncle could live in his bubble of luxury and pretend he was important.

How she hated him.

"Be gone with you," Uncle Charlie said, pinching the bridge of his nose "You are giving me a headache."

Considering she had hardly uttered a word, she wasn't certain how she had managed that, but she scurried away anyway, stepping through the hallway and straight into the snug comfort of her aunt's room. A fire offered fingers of warmth and she stepped gratefully toward it, spreading her palms out with the hope the heat could chase away the chill that interactions with her uncle and Mr. Worthington left her with.

The door opened behind her and she spun and clamped her hands behind her back, feeling as though she had been caught doing something naughty. Of course, it was her aunt and not her uncle. Who else would it be? Grace relaxed her posture and dashed toward her.

Aunt Elsie was only slightly taller than her but softer, and oh so, comforting. Since she'd come here at the age of eight, her aunt's embrace had always helped soothe away any troubles.

Except there was nothing a comforting embrace could do now.

"I was listening at the door," her aunt told her, her voice low.

Grace eased away so she could view her aunt's worried expression. Aunt Elsie reminded her of her father with faded red hair and a clear emerald gaze. She even had the same strong eyebrows. Her patient and calm temperament had been shared by Grace's father too.

"You know they want me to marry him before my birthday then."

Aunt Elsie nodded. "But we shall not let that happen."

"How? I cannot even think—"

Her aunt clasped her arms. "Shh." She glanced around the room. "I have a plan. It is a little wild, but it shall work. I promise."

Chapter Two

"Dash it all." Nash rubbed the sore spot on his head that would likely be bruised by tomorrow. He glared at the low beam responsible for his injury then ducked into the cramped front room of the cottage. At least a fire was roaring in the grate, popping and spitting its warmth into a room too small for three grown men.

Nevertheless, they were all standing in it, looking like giants inside a child's doll's house. He swore, once he got his fortune from his father, he was going to spend money on a new meeting place for them—some cottage elsewhere with generous rooms and no bloody beams.

"Every time," said Guy with a smirk.

"I'm going to carve a hole out of that beam," Nash threatened, gesturing to the offending bit of wood.

Hawthorne Cottage had been their meeting place for nigh on two years owing to its isolated state and relative proximity to his Shropshire estate.

Though, estate was putting it kindly. When one mentioned an estate, one thought of sweeping fields, pristine lawns, maybe a few deer sheltering under trees. Guildham House was far from that.

He'd change that too once he got his money. Just like he'd always dreamed.

"Firstly, I think Mrs. Heath would be none too happy if you did such a thing and, secondly, I'm fairly certain you'd bring the ceiling down upon us." The Earl of Henleigh jabbed the ceiling above and a little plaster came away.

"I don't think one beam is holding this ceiling up." Nash grimaced as he glanced at the water-stained, patchy ceiling. "In fact, I'm not certain anything is holding it up." He flung himself into the threadbare armchair that was nestled in one corner of the room, close enough to the fire that he could prop his feet on the tiles surrounding it and dry his damp boots. "We should find a new meeting place," he declared.

Russell shook his head and remained standing while Guy followed Nash's suit and settled on the other armchair. Marcus Russell was the tallest of them all and practically had to stoop to be standing in this room.

"This house is just fine." Russell tugged off his gloves and laid them across his lap. "Cheap, good location, and far from prying eyes."

"Not to mention, completely unconnected to us," Guy pointed out.

Nash waved a hand. "There must be hundreds of isolated cottages for let. I do not see why we can't maintain our privacy in a more comfortable location."

Guy lifted a dark brow. The marquis had likely perfected that look and used it to his advantage many a time, but Nash ignored it. If he was one to be cowed by a mere eyebrow, he'd have rolled over and played dead years ago when his father threatened to cut him off. "I thought you were all for ensuring we make as much profit out of this venture as possible."

"I have my needs, I will admit." Nash eyed his fingernails and frowned at the ragged appearance of his ring finger. *Not* the fingers of a viscount-to-be.

No. An eventual viscount-to-be.

A viscount-to-be who would likely be waiting another twenty years. Which meant, in the meantime, he needed coin, and he had no desire to make his nails any more ragged than they already were. His venture with Russell and Guy was a perfect way to ensure he could survive until such a day that he inherited the title and all the entailed estates.

He sighed. "Fine, I shall tolerate this cottage a little longer."

"How lucky we are," Guy said with a wry grin.

"You damn well are lucky. Without me, you'd have nowhere to stash the girls."

"We'd manage," muttered Russell.

"And no one to look after them." Nash pointed to Guy. "You are far too busy with all your earl-ish business to spend weeks caring for poor, weeping, heartbroken women. And you," he thrust a finger at Russell, "wouldn't know what to do with a crying woman. He'd probably make her cry more," he said to Guy.

Russell straightened. "I've dealt with a crying woman before. Plenty of them cry on the journey."

"Funnily enough, they're usually still crying by the time they reach me." Nash leaned forward. "How exactly did you deal with them?"

"Well, I—"

"Enough," ordered Guy. "We have business of which to attend, and nothing is going to change. This will remain our meeting place and Russell will continue to deliver the women—crying or not—whilst Nash looks after them."

Russell glowered at Nash while he grinned boldly. Oh, how he loved to jest with him. It was the only way to make him seem human sometimes. He always had an odd, sort of uncaring attitude to him, as though he would be happy to put up his feet anywhere and go to sleep. He rarely unleashed any emotion—with the exception of a fiery temper that seemed to come from nowhere.

Nash didn't know much about the man, aside from the fact he was loyal to a fault and a damn good fighter. Thankfully, Nash had never ended up on the wrong end of Russell's fists, but the tall Welshman had got them out of a sticky situation a time or two with great ease.

Not that Nash was any kind of pacifist and had wound up in a brawl or two in his lifetime, but he'd far rather have Russell on his side than not.

Guy dashed a hand through brown hair that looked like it was due a cut. The stubble on his jaw was decidedly un-earl like too. What was going on in Lord Guy's life, Nash could not say. They had been friends since before college but once he had inherited his title and started this kidnap lark, the earl hardly had a second to spare. Nash would suggest taking on a wife to share the burden, but Guy steered clear of women since that bloody awful Eleanor had shattered the man's heart.

Nash, on the other hand, had all the time in the world to spare. He was just counting down the days until his father died and he could prove to the old stick he wasn't as bad as his father feared. Had he gambled a small fortune away? Admittedly, yes.

But had he also been utterly prepared to change his ways once he inherited? Well, perhaps not at the time. But things were different. Especially now he was damned poor.

Nash still didn't think it was a good reason to cut one's only son off. After all, there were plenty of lords to be out there who did far worse than spend a little time in gaming hells.

"So who is the woman this time?" asked Russell.

"A Miss Grace Beaumont," said Guy.

Grace Beaumont. Pale haired, rosy cheeked. Curves a plenty. Wide eyes. Of course, he had no idea who the woman was but that was how he pictured her. "And the reason we are helping her?"

"Something to do with escaping a fiancé. The man was known to be violent with his wife," Guy explained.

"Bastard," hissed Russell.

Nash leaned forward. "Is she attractive?"

Guy rolled his eyes while Russell gave an annoyed grunt.

"What?" Nash lifted his hands. "I have to know what the girl I'm looking after looks like or else I might get the wrong damned girl!"

Russell peered down at him. "You have to know what the girl—who I am handing directly to you—looks like? For fear I might be handing you the wrong girl?"

He shrugged. "It could happen."

"It doesn't matter anyway," Guy said. "I didn't meet her."

"Who did you meet?" Nash demanded.

"The aunt. She's the one arranging it. Heard about us from Lady Smythe. We helped her cousin if you recall."

Nash nodded. Lady Smythe's cousin had spent many a day crying whilst he watched over her before she was dispatched to Ireland. She was a sweet thing, though, and he didn't much mind comforting a crying woman. If there was nothing else he could do with his time, he might as well offer his broad shoulders for some use.

"What of the aunt?" Nash asked.

Guy frowned. "What of her?"

"Is she attractive?"

"Good Lord, Nash, she was thirty years my senior."

Nash lifted his shoulders. "I'm an equal opportunities lover."

Guy thrust a finger his way. "You will be avoiding all opportunities of being a lover or you'll be out," he warned him.

"Yes, yes, I know."

There was no chance Nash would give up this easy way of earning money nor being part of The Kidnap Club, as they had deemed themselves.

Admittedly, he had the least exciting part of the job, watching over the women whilst their escapes were planned, or finances were organized, or lovers were brought to them for elopement. He suspected Russell had the best part, taking the women then protecting them on the road, but he was happy to put his forgotten and neglected estate to use, and he didn't have to worry about armed drivers deciding their jobs were worth more than their lives and letting off a few shots.

Nash folded his arms and grinned. "Sometimes I think you only want me for my house."

Guy's brows lifted. "That's precisely why we want you."

"You know how to make a man feel loved," he grumbled.

"The girl," Russell pressed. "What of her?"

"We shall be kidnapping her in two days' time. She'll be on the road, travelling to see a friend in Somerset with her aunt. That's when we'll take her."

"You said the aunt organized this. The girl does know what is going to happen, does she not?" asked Russell.

Guy nodded. "She knows all about it."

Nash laced his fingers together and leaned back, looping his hands behind his back. "What will we be doing with her? Escorting her to some spinster aunt in the middle of nowhere? Sending her to Gretna with a lover?"

Guy shook his head. "We're going to ruin her."

Nash nearly choked on his next breath.

"What the devil?" said Russell under his breath.

Nash peered at Guy, wondering now if the long hair and unkempt appearance was a sign of madness rather than busyness. When Guy had brought him onboard to help a cousin of his escape an awful marriage and it had become clear there was a need for their strange sort of service, there had been strict orders of no ruining. Not even any kissing. Nash was to be as uncharming as possible.

A tough feat indeed but he had managed it thus far.

"Miss Beaumont is an heiress. She inherits all her money as soon as she turns one and twenty—in just over a month's time. At which point, she is entirely independent. The plan is to hold her for ransom until she is of age then we'll deposit her back in London, older and most likely 'ruined' by one of the kidnappers. Her fiancé-to-be will lose interest and she will be free of him."

Russell hissed out a breath. "This sounds dangerous, Guy. Hold her for a whole month?"

"Indeed," Nash agreed. "We've never held a woman for more than two weeks. We'd better be getting paid a fortune for this."

Guy made a face and Russell groaned. "What is it?"

"We will get paid. Twice actually."

Nash clapped his hands together. "Sounds perfect. I like it."

"Once the ransom is paid and once again when Miss Beaumont gets her inheritance."

"The ransom?" echoed Russell.

"No," said Nash. "Recall the last time we tried to collect on a ransom? They are for guise only, you always said that. To keep people on their toes and ensure no one hunts the women."

Russell nodded. "No ransoms you said, even if we demanded them."

Guy held out both hands. "Let us just say, that although Miss Beaumont is an heiress, she is still a woman of simple means. She cannot afford our fee."

"And you only said one charity case a year," pointed out Russell. "We need that money or else we can't continue doing this. At least Nash and I do."

"I know, I know." Guy rubbed a hand across his chin. "The ransom will be more than enough."

"If the ransom can be paid by her family, why isn't the aunt simply paying our fee?" Russell queried.

"The aunt is poor. The uncle is not. He'll pay it, she is certain, just to get his niece back so he can wed her off."

A headache was beginning to start behind Nash's eyes. Even if Miss Beaumont was fair-haired and rosy-cheeked, she might not be worth this much danger. "And when we don't return her? How can we guarantee they won't try to come after us?"

"We cannot," Guy admitted. "But we are careful. We always have been. No one will track her to your estate, and this will be over before we know it."

Nash rubbed his forehead. "You had better hope she is worth it, Guy. I have little intention of being strung up over this Miss Grace Beaumont."

Even if she was the prettiest girl in the world.

Chapter Three

It was hard to decide whether to be horrified or excited by this whole 'kidnapping' matter.

Was she addled to go through with this?

Probably.

Desperate too.

Grace eyed the unfamiliar countryside passing by at a rapid pace and clutched the cat tighter to her. Claude wriggled in protest and she released the animal. He stretched, took a dainty step off her lap, and twisted around several times before settling on the cushion beside her. She wished she could feel so at ease having been bundled into this stranger's carriage by a masked man with long legs, and little to say for himself.

She understood the urgency, really she did, but she'd rather hoped for a few words of comfort from her kidnapper.

Horrified. That's what she should be.

The whole matter had been such a strange, swift affair. The man had held up the carriage in which she'd been travelling with her aunt and taken her away at gunpoint in mere seconds. Her aunt did a fine job of playing distressed, but Grace was not so certain her own acting had been convincing. Especially when she'd refused to part with Claude.

The cat had been with her for years and as dismissive of her as the cat seemed now, he needed her.

And she needed him. If she was going to embark on this madcap plan, she needed her cat. Needed at least one familiar thing, considering she had left all her worldly belongings behind—what few she had that was.

It was a little exciting, though. She was leaving the awful Mr. Worthington behind and escaping her uncle's clutches. It was like an adventure story, even if she did envisage her time away to be rather dull. She was not entirely sure what to expect but it sounded much like she would pass her days hunkered down, just making sure no one found her.

Hopefully, wherever it was she was to stay was not too uncomfortable or boring but having lived with her uncle, she had grown used to existing on little while he hoarded whatever he could for his own luxurious lifestyle. These days, she was lucky to own even a single book as most of them had been sold or were used to ensure his room looked the part.

The carriage hit a bump in the road, and she gripped the edge of the window. Claude opened an eye, twisted around, and resettled.

"It's all very well for you," she muttered to him.

How lovely it must be to be a cat. Nothing to worry about apart from where the comfiest cushion was. No fears of what might be ahead.

Good Lord, what was she doing? She never did anything different or unusual. She certainly never put her fate in the hands of strangers, especially for money. What if he intended to harm her? What if they wanted more money? There were so many things that could go wrong, and this was the most foolish, illogical thing anyone could ever do.

Horrifying, most definitely.

What woman in her right mind would go through with such a thing?

But, according to her aunt, these men were practiced in this and entirely trustworthy. She said an important man led the whole thing. Why an *important man* would wish to get involved with ransoms, and kidnappings, and helping women escape their fates she did not know, but how angry it made her that there was such a need for this service.

She frowned to herself. If it could be called a 'service.' It seemed a little silly to name it such a thing but what else could one call it?

If only the masked man had stopped to tell her where they were going or how long they would be travelling. They had been on the road for at least three hours and the interior of the carriage was growing cold. A blanket had been provided but it was thin and threadbare. She hoped this was not indicative of the care she was going to endure over the next month. She was no prissy, demanding lady but she loathed being cold.

At least the rain had stayed away, she supposed. Gray clouds had hung over the day like an ominous sign. Wet roads would have made the travelling all the harder and presumably made their already long journey much longer. She only hoped they were nearing the end.

Hauling the blanket a little higher, she shook her head at Claude. "The least you could do is sit on my lap and keep me warm."

Claude ignored her, apparently sleeping, though Grace was certain she'd seen one eye slide open oh so briefly.

Grace shook her head and gave the cat a quick pet then returned her attention to the road outside. Lines of barren trees passed by before giving way to open land. Fields stretched out for some distance with no sign of life anywhere. Everything was tinged a dark gray by the threatening sky so that even the rolling hills looked unwelcome. They passed a tall pile of stone, set at odd angles and with chunks missing, and she realized it must have once been an entrance arch. Perhaps they were nearly there.

How exciting.

She craned her neck to see ahead, pressing her forehead against the glass of the window. The road continued down a hill then curved up a little. It wasn't until they reached the brow of the hill did she see the building ahead. A huge house sat nestled in the valley, silhouetted against the hills behind it.

A shiver ran down her spine. The dark windows looked like little demon's eyes, all black and emotionless. Even from here, she could tell the house was not lived in. The grand building offered up an air of neglect with untidy lawns, scrawny trees and bare vines wrapped around stone.

Horrifying. Most Definitely Horrifying.

UGLY. MOST DEFINITELY ugly.

Hairy too but not necessarily in the right places. Bald patches provided a strange pale pink contrast to the black and white tufts.

Nash peered around the cat, currently held at arm's length by Russell. "What is this?"

Russell shrugged, his expression masked by the cloth covering his mouth and nose. "She insisted."

"You were kidnapping her. How the devil did she find time to insist?"

Russell shrugged again, offering the cat forward once more. The animal blinked lazily at him, apparently unbothered by the long journey and the man holding him. Nash took it and glanced the wretched creature over. As ugly as it was, it looked clean, though he still could not fathom what sort of a woman would insist on bringing a scraggy thing like this on a kidnapping.

"Don't put Claude down," a woman commanded. "He'll run away."

Claude?

Russell stepped aside and a child clambered down from the carriage. Nash blinked several times and looked to Russell. *That's her?* he mouthed. Russell nodded.

Nash glanced her over. He knew her to be twenty but her slight appearance had him deceived for a moment. Everything about her was tiny. Small, pursed lips, delicate chin, little pinched nose. He reckoned he could span her waist with both hands, and he made that judgement even with the added weight of her cloak. The only thing that wasn't small about her was her wide, dark eyes that seemed to take everything in. Her gaze darted up to the pediment above him, down to the steps on which he stood, and back to him, skimming up and down him a few times.

Small for certain.

Not ugly, though.

Unlike... "Claude?"

She nodded and opened her arms. "The cat."

He handed the creature over and watched while she fussed over it, cooing words that didn't sound right at all muttered to such a scruffy thing. Things like *darling boy*, and *cute baby*. He wrinkled his nose. How anyone could love such an animal, he did not know.

"Well, I shall leave you to it," announced Russell. "All went well, and we weren't followed."

Nash was half-tempted to try to persuade Russell to stay. He couldn't say why but there was something disturbing about this Miss Beaumont. Or perhaps it was just the cat that threw him off.

For goodness sake's anyone would think he had never seen a cat or a vaguely pretty woman before. He cleared his throat and clasped his hands behind his back, forcing a charming smile across his lips.

"I'll get Miss Beaumont settled."

"Right you are." Russell tipped his hat and climbed back into the driver's seat.

"Mary will be here any moment," Nash said.

Miss Beaumont clutched the cat tightly to her, her eyes still wide. "Mary?"

"She will cook and help care for you."

"What are you to do?"

"I'm your protector, of course."

She tilted her head. "Do I need protection? I thought the idea was no one would find me here."

No one had ever traced any of the women to this house, that was true. It was so old, remote and forgotten, not many knew it ever existed. With the exception of a few very trusted people to help keep them fed and warm, of course.

That did not mean, however, the women could be left alone. Sometimes they wanted to change their mind and go home. Other times, they begged to go visit a friend or a relative, and he was the one who had to persuade them to stick to the plan. Thankfully, he was a persuasive sort of a person.

"No one will find you," he promised. He gestured up at the house. "I am here for your protection and because this is my house."

She blinked a few times. "It is...um...a little tired."

He laughed. "You could say that. But it works perfectly for our purposes."

"I see."

"Come in, no doubt you are tired after your journey, and..." He sighed. "Bring the creature with you."

"Claude," she corrected. "As in *clawed*." She wrinkled her nose. "It's supposed to be funny."

"Claude," he muttered, leading her through the front doors. "Hilarious."

He knew how the house had to look to her eyes. It didn't look any different to him. There was no housekeeper to keep it organized, no scullery maids, no butlers. Dust coated the bannister and dry leaves gathered in corners of the entrance hall. If his father had not cut him off, it would look vastly different but as it was, he could not fund keeping it maintained.

Yet.

Regardless, he loved the old building. He always had. He glanced over his shoulder to find her frozen in the middle of the room. The vast ceiling that led all the way up to a grimy glass dome made her look even more petite. She looked up at the dome for a few moments then met his gaze. "This was once a fine house."

"It was."

"I do not know your name."

He smiled. Silly of him. He hadn't even introduced himself. Something was definitely strange about this meeting. Normally the women welcomed a strong man to protect them and soothe any worries. Miss Beaumont simply seemed nonplussed by the whole situation.

"Nash."

"Just Nash?"

"It is better you know me only by that name."

"I see." She blew out a breath. "I suppose that is quite logical. What you do must be dangerous."

"Oh yes." He flashed a smile.

She tilted her head. "I cannot fathom why you should want to put yourself in danger."

"I like to help women in need."

A brow rose and she pursed her lips. She took a few methodical paces around the room, inspecting a dusty statue of David and a portrait of Wickstead Castle, his ancestral home. Finally, she turned her attention back to him. "You may call me Grace then, I suppose. It would be silly to use formalities on the woman you kidnapped."

He nodded. "Grace it is." He gestured upstairs. "Shall we get you settled?"

Grace glanced at the door and he suspected she was debating whether to escape or go through with their plan. He couldn't make this woman out yet but clearly she was not entirely at peace with her decision to flee her engagement.

Maybe the aunt was wrong? Maybe Grace cared for the blaggard?

Well, it didn't matter either way. He had one job to do and he'd damn well do it so they could see a good payday. Then maybe he could finally pay someone to clean the house.

"Very well," she said tightly. "Show me my room."

Chapter Four

Nash glanced around for Mary but suspected she was working in the kitchen. Even though there was only the two of them, he always relied on Mary for aid. Mostly because if it was down to him to feed the captive, the most he could conjure up was a slab of bread.

Much of the time, the women were wealthy too, and used to being served. It helped to have Mary to unlace dresses and whatnot. Not that he minded unlacing a beautiful woman's dress, but he'd vowed to Guy he'd maintain a professional courtesy. It did mean he sometimes had to turn down the odd advance, but he doubted he'd have anything to worry about with this wide-eyed, wary woman who spoke so plainly.

Her feet upon the steps barely made a sound as she followed him to the bedrooms. He indicated down the hallway. "We keep the two wings closed off to ensure this part of the building stays warm. You will sleep here." He pushed open a door just to the left of the stairs.

Though it still suffered an air of neglect Mary kept it clean and warm. He loved this room. He still recalled hiding from his older sister in here as a boy and getting a severe scolding when they could not find him for a whole afternoon.

A fire suffused the room with warmth and a generous carved wooden bed strung with thick red curtains offered an appealing sanctuary.

Grace finally lowered the cat to the floor and straightened. She fingered the gold fabric-covered walls. "Where will you be sleeping?"

He hesitated. He wasn't unused to the question but had not expected it from her. She certainly did not seem the sort to need to dash to his bedroom in the middle of the night because she heard a noise—despite her delicate appearance.

"Two rooms down." He jerked his head to the right.

"I see."

Nash watched the cat sniff a certain spot on the carpet then stroll casually over to one of the lengths of curtain and lift its tail.

"Claude, no!" She snatched the cat up and tapped his nose with what Nash could only think of as an affectionate tap.

"Did it just...relieve itself on the curtains?"

She grimaced. "I am sorry. He is just trying to make himself at home."

"Could he not do that by—I don't know—sleeping on the bed or something?"

"That is not how cats work, I am afraid. Especially male ones."

Nash folded his arms. "He can't sleep in here. Not if he's going to *urinate* everywhere."

"He won't, I promise." She clasped the cat tightly to her.

"He can stay in the kitchen. There will be rats to catch down there no doubt. Put him to good use."

Her eyes widened further if that was possible. "No! I need him with me."

"Miss Beaumont—Grace—I do not make a habit of allowing animals in my house. Especially cats. I really think—"

"Wait. Do you not like cats?"

"I like them. When they are in my kitchens, doing what they were obviously put on the earth to do."

"So you don't like them then."

"Does it matter?"

"Of course it does. You are missing out on everything cats can offer! Did you know that their purring can act to soothe almost any ailment?"

He resisted the desire to scrub a hand over his face. Could she not have come here wailing and weeping about whatever it was she had left behind? No, instead she was lecturing him on the benefits of animals of the feline variety.

"I very much doubt—"

"Not to mention they are warm and perfect bed companions."

Clearly, she had never had anyone in her bed apart from a cat because that was wholly wrong.

"And they are clean creatures. They take minimal care. A little food every now and then and they still give you all their love."

He eyed the docile animal, its arms splayed over her one arm, the little claws at the tips of his white paws visible. The cat blinked and yawned as though talking of his many wonderful traits was dull indeed and he had heard this lecture a hundred times. No doubt his owner often extolled his virtues.

Nash sighed and gave into curiosity. "Why is he bald in places anyway?"

"I rescued him from a river," she said proudly, "and we have never been apart for a day since."

He hardly knew Miss Grace Beaumont but, somehow, he could picture this tiny woman stripping away her cloak and diving into the most furious of rivers just to save this ugly cat.

"That still doesn't explain the bald patches."

She lifted a shoulder and placed him on the bed. "He must have had a hard life, but he's never told me about it."

Oh dear. Maybe she was simple. Or addled. Perhaps the kidnapping experience had shocked her so much that she thought she could talk to animals.

"He...he talks to you?"

She laughed as though he was silly indeed. He had to admit, he rather liked it when she smiled. Much better than that strange, nonplussed look she constantly wore. However, he wasn't certain he liked her laughing at him.

"Of course not! But when you get to know an animal, you can usually understand their story. He hates water, which is normal for cats, of course, but he is deathly afraid of it. Sometimes one can tell what they have experienced in their past from their behavior now. Much like humans I suppose." She looked at him and her gaze narrowed slightly, as though she were trying to figure out his story.

Not that he had much of one. Rich, privileged, and then it was all torn away from him by his father. Now he was just biding his time until he was rich and privileged again.

"You should pet him," she said.

"No."

"But you might like it."

"I am quite happy appreciating all Claude has to offer from a distance thank you. Besides, we had a good...cuddle earlier when you arrived."

Her lips quirked a little. "I will never understand why the stronger sex is afraid of cats."

"I am certainly not afraid."

"Very well. If you say so."

"I do say so," he said firmly.

"Of course." Her smile told him she did not believe him.

A tap at the door prevented him from arguing further and Mary popped her head around the door. "Good evening! I thought I heard the carriage arrive."

"You did indeed." Nash backed away. At least Mary saved him from being forced into touching the scraggy cat. "I shall leave you in Mary's capable hands."

He dipped his head and hastened out of the room, shaking his head to himself. Miss Beaumont was not the usual kidnapee that was for certain.

GRACE COULD NOT help but stare at the empty space where Nash had been standing. This whole process had been disconcerting enough without someone like...like him being in charge of her protection or whatever it was he did.

Disconcerting was a good way of describing him. He had all the strength one could ask for from a protector that was clear enough. He towered over her which was nothing new but broad shoulders filled a jacket that was a few seasons out of style.

The only reason she knew that was because her uncle was forever espousing the benefits of remaining in fashion. Not that she had worn a fashionable thing in her life, nor did she want to. Practical, comfortable clothing was more her thing, and she did not much enjoy low-cut gowns that revealed her minimal assets or tight waistlines or itchy lace. Give her some plain muslin and a fichu any day.

Her gaze strayed back to the empty space where she half-expected there to be boot indents in the carpet from his sheer presence. She did not know much about the opposite sex, but she recognized a self-confident man when she saw one.

Mr. Worthington had a similar air except he would never admit to being scared of cats. Not that Nash had exactly admitted it, but the fear was there, lingering behind sage green eyes. She rather liked that fear even if she did not understand it. It made him more human than Mr. Worthington, despite his ridiculously attractive appearance.

Mary shut the door behind her and hastened forward. "You poor thing, you must be frozen."

Actually, she was just fine. Hot even. And not just because of the fire in the room and the cozy furnishings. Nash had left her cheeks heated when she thought of how handsome he was. It made sense, she supposed, that these sorts of things occurred. After all, she was a woman in her prime. Her body was readying her for having babies and what better way for nature to persuade her to do such a thing than ensure she was attracted to a specimen of the opposite sex. Attraction was part of being human, most naturally.

If only she could naturally ignore that lure. But the way his almost black hair curled just so around his ears and touched his nape made her fingers tingle, and when she thought of his mouth—strong but with generous lips, her breathing grew agitated.

Human nature had a lot to answer to.

"We shall get a good meal in you shortly." Mary unfastened Grace's cloak. "Not to worry, I know you came here with nothing. Apart from the cat it seems. But we have plenty of clothing for the girls, much of it fine indeed, donated by some of the other ladies we've helped." Mary glanced her over. "Though you are such a tiny thing. I may have to do a few clever stitches."

Grace opened her mouth then closed it. It was so strange to think other women had done the same, stood in the exact same position as her. They had probably pondered the handsomeness of Nash too. How did such a man end up providing this service? How did any of them?

She watched Mary fold her cloak and retrieve a gown from a large blanket box with a latch on it that reminded her of a treasure box. Though not much taller than herself, Mary was curvier and probably a few years older than her. She had ginger hair and lashes to match that made the blue of her eyes more stark against her pale, freckled skin.

Her face was slender, coming to a strong point at her chin. Her features seemed at odds with her warm tone and motherly movements—it felt as though she should have a generous bosom and warm, apple red cheeks.

"This is nice and thick and not too large. We may just have to tie something about your waist. Shall I help you change for dinner?"

"Dinner?" Grace echoed.

Mary smiled. "You have had a long, tiring day. You need food," she said softly.

Grace considered her body, aware it ached from the carriage ride but unable to fathom if she was hungry or not. "I had better eat I suppose."

"Quite right, keep your strength up. Now about your gown..."

"I can manage myself, thank you. I...I never had a maid." She wasn't certain why it made her feel silly to admit that—maybe it was because she was standing in what was once a grand house indeed and she imagined any woman staying here would have brought an entire entourage. Whatever it was, she felt out of place and entirely out of her depth.

Mary put a hand to her arm. "I know this has been a strange experience, but Nash is a kind man and will look after you well." She bent and gave the fire a quick prod with a poker. "And I am here most afternoons."

"Oh. You are not here all the time?"

She shook her head. "I only help when I am needed, and it would not be very good money if I did not help at the farm."

"I see."

"Please do not worry. Nash looks like a rake and I've no doubt he was once, but he will be a gentleman."

Grace shook her head vaguely. "I am not worried about him."

At least, she thought she wasn't. *He would not want someone like me anyway.*

Without her inheritance, not even Mr. Worthington would want her. But, she had to admit, there was something strange twisting in her gut about the idea of being alone with him. Maybe it was simply because he was unknown to her.

That made sense really. Humans were designed not to like new things or strangers, it was a matter of survival really. She just had to convince her instincts that they did not need to be functioning right now.

"Well, I shall leave you to dress. We don't ring a dinner gong here so be sure to be down by seven."

"Oh, where is the dining room?"

"Downstairs, turn right and go through the first parlor room."

Grace twined her hands together. "Will, um, Nash be there too?"

"He's a man and he always wants feeding so, yes."

"Oh. Yes. Good. Of course." Grace wanted to hide her face in her hands. How addled her mind was. What did she expect? That he might hide himself away at dinner and leave her eating alone at some grand table? She needed to get a grip of herself. And fast.

Chapter Five

"Shoo."

Nash followed the sound of urgent *shoos*. Several more followed before he came upon Grace by the rear steps of the house. Skirts clutched in one hand, she frantically waved a hand at the peacock and took a step back.

"Shoo, I tell you."

The peacock, entirely unperturbed by her commands, ruffled his spread of feathers. Apparently, the bird thought Grace was worthy of a display and didn't realize she was most certainly uninterested. She took a sudden step forward then darted back when the bird moved closer.

"I would never harm you but, please, you must leave me be," she begged the bird.

Nash folded his arms and watched the exhibition, his lips curved. He didn't blame the creature for wanting to impress her. Though he supposed her figure verged on boyish, in the morning sunlight that had forced its way through cracks in the thick clouds, the pretty tilt of her chin was all the more evident.

He'd not been unaware of her attractiveness at dinner, but it had been somewhat tarnished by her abrupt manner. There was no coquettishness to her, no gentleness. Miss Beaumont asked questions directly and didn't seem to understand if one wished to skirt around the question or answer in some way other than direct.

For some reason, fighting a peacock made her vastly more attractive. Pinned up loosely, her coal-black hair enhanced the pale tint of her skin. Little loose strands touched her face and she blew one away, making his fingers twitch.

"Please," she urged the bird. "Leave me be."

Her voice cracked a little—Nash's call to aid. He strode forward and stepped between her and the peacock. "Priscilla, be gone," he ordered firmly. "Off with you."

The bird ruffled his feathers, gave him what could only be considered a cold look and slowly turned, making sure they got a full view of his display before he sauntered off toward the overgrown wilds of the formal gardens.

He turned to Grace who was halfway up the stairs, clinging to the stone balustrade. "Are you well?"

She nodded, inhaled deeply, and unwound herself from the bannister. "I am well." She glanced after the bird. "Priscilla? But he's a he."

He chuckled. "He was given to us as a baby and we did not realize he was a boy until he was older and colorful. By then, the name had stuck."

"Why on earth do you keep him here of all places?"

"As you can see, he makes an excellent guard."

She pressed a hand to her chest and straightened. "Animals normally like me."

"Well, Priscilla is a bird. And I would say he really liked you."

"He had a strange way of showing it."

Nash lifted a shoulder. "That's most men I'm afraid. We're always trying to impress the ladies, but we go about it in the clumsiest of manners."

She peered up at him. The sun had given up trying to defeat the clouds, leaving the day slightly overcast. But apparently the sun could not be given full credit for making Grace appear pretty. Her clear dark eyes, framed by black, long lashes were captivating, forcing him to stare into them far longer than was polite. She didn't seem to notice and studied him in return until a shriek from Priscilla broke the spell.

"I imagine you are never clumsy," she finally said.

"I have my moments."

A lie.

He wasn't certain why he was downplaying his skills with women, but it felt needed.

"No, I do not think you do."

Well, apparently, she saw through his lie. He would have to remember that.

"What were you doing when you came upon Priscilla?"

"I wished to explore the grounds. I tried to explore the house a little last night, but it was too dark, and you have most of it shut off."

"I can show you more during your stay but as I said, we do it so we do not have to heat too many rooms."

"Do you live here all the time?" she asked.

"I stay with friends a fair bit."

She came down from her steps to stand right in front of him. "In Town?"

"Mostly, yes."

"Why do you live here?" She glanced around the gardens.

He knew what she saw. Overgrown vines, dead rose bushes, uneven trees, stone benches crawling with ivy. A far cry from the grand place it once had been.

"It is a long story."

"We have time," she pointed out.

"A boring one then."

And not really all that long but the last thing he wanted to do was moan about his father or admit his past discrepancies to her.

He frowned. Why though?

Gads, for some inane reason, he wanted to impress her.

Nash indicated down the path that led between tall, unkempt box trees. "Shall we explore together?"

"I..." She blinked at him a few times. "Yes, that would be acceptable."

"Excellent." He grinned and clasped his hands behind his back. "I can protect you from Priscilla should he decide to renew his interests."

"I do not know why he did not like me."

"As I said, he liked you too much."

"I always felt I had an affinity with all of God's creatures," she admitted. "I suppose I have not met them all, but I have never met one that I could not charm."

Rather like him and women but Grace had yet to fall for his charms. Perhaps she was his Priscilla. Though, she was certainly not putting on bright displays. In fact, rather the opposite. Her quiet, methodical ways were a far cry from how women usually behaved around him.

They strolled between the trees. Overgrown grass caught on the hem of her skirts and she lifted them slightly, giving him the faintest view of a stockinged ankle. He moved his gaze swiftly. He'd managed to resist many a woman staying here and this one would be no different.

So why the devil was a mere glimpse of a tiny ankle—a tiny, fabric covered ankle—making him feel all hot and bothered?

GRACE FROWNED. WHY had his gaze darted away like that when she'd glanced at him? His posture stiffened too. Had she said something wrong? It would not be unusual for her. Thanks to her uncle's miserly ways—at least when it came to her and her aunt—she seldom socialized and her father had been keen for her to spend her time studying at his side rather than watching the local ladies go to tea and don pretty gowns. So her ability to indulge in light conversation was at a minimum.

Still, she did not think she had said anything too odd.

She peered up at the overgrown trees surrounding them. She had so much to ask. She wanted that long story behind why he had come to live here, why it was so unkempt. In a way, it was the most marvelous house she had ever seen. The wild vines, the old, broken trees, the green-tinged windows, and the tired furnishings all held such a story and it interested her to no end.

But despite seeming easy to converse with, Nash was surprisingly reserved when it came to talk of himself. She had managed to summon the courage to pepper him with questions at dinner last night, but he had evaded most of them.

She opened her mouth then shut it. How did a man like Nash come to be involved in such an odd arrangement? Sadly, she understood all too well the need for women to disappear.

Now she knew of this strange group of men, she had to wonder if they had been involved in the few disappearances of society ladies from miserable marriages.

What a history they must have! And why oh why did they even start such a thing? She wished she'd brought her notepad with her so she could jot down some notes, perhaps glean something from the small amount he had told her.

Maybe if she asked Mary, she might be able to find something for her to write on. She always did her best thinking on paper—much, much easier than talking aloud. She always thought how much easier it would be if life could be conducted fully by letter. She'd like to give her uncle a good scolding and tell him what a nasty toad she thought he was. Unfortunately, in person, she could never summon such courage.

"How is Claude settling in?" Nash asked.

"Mary gave him some fish this morning and he seemed content indeed. I've left him in my room. Cats need time to discover their surroundings or else they have a tendency to get lost."

"I thought cats were the easy-to-care-for sort?"

"Well, I hardly think shutting him in my room is hard work. Besides, he will sleep quite happily all day."

"So long as he doesn't decide to urinate on anything else."

"He was just trying to make himself comfortable."

A dark brow rose. "If I urinated everywhere I wanted to make myself comfortable, I would be banished from most places."

"He has some straw to do it on now. He's quite clean, honestly. I taught him myself."

"Did you also teach him to piss on curtains?"

She opened her mouth again. Then shook her head.

"Forgive my poor language. I did not mean to shock you."

"Oh no, I am not shocked. Actually, my father espoused the use of crass language. He imagined it to be a sign of intelligence. Besides, when one limits one's language, surely one is limiting one's thinking ability too?"

He eyed her, his lips curving. "I'm not certain about that but I suppose I never saw the harm in the odd curse or two. Most ladies do not appreciate it, however."

"Oh." He must have forgotten he was with a lady. She was no-one special, but she had good breeding and her uncle was well-respected. Once she had her inheritance, she would be considered to have middling wealth—enough for a few people to pay attention to and certainly enough for her to live comfortably with her aunt for the rest of their days.

But she was not like other ladies, so she did not blame him. She had no charms, no tricks with fans, no coquettish looks or assets with which to attract him.

Not that she wanted to. Good Lord, no. It was ridiculous enough that she was having to pretend to be kidnapped to escape Mr. Worthington. Thinking she might somehow lure this man with whatever she had to offer was verging on insane.

And, of course, she had no desire to lure him. Or anyone for that matter.

"You can cry if you want."

Grace paused and cocked her head. "Cry?"

"If you want." He tugged out a handkerchief and offered it to her. "I can even offer an embrace if you'd like. I've been told I'm quite good at them." His cocky smile made her scowl.

"I do not understand."

"Most women cry. When they come here. It is a trying time for them."

"It is a strange thing to be sure but..."

"Perhaps running from your fiancé has been upsetting. I would completely understand." He offered the handkerchief again.

"He is not my fiancé. At least not to my mind. I never once accepted him," she said firmly.

His brows rose. "I see."

"And if I were to be so weak as to cry over such an awful man, I should be angry with myself indeed." She folded her arms across her chest. "I am not weak, no matter how I appear."

He held up both palms. "I did not think it for one second."

"Oh."

"I just thought you might need some comforting. You seemed a little out of sorts."

She let her shoulders relax. "I am often out of sorts, Nash. I am afraid this is just the way I am."

"So...no crying?"

She shook her head vigorously. "Never."

He studied her for a moment, running his gaze from her head to her toes then back again before shaking his head. "Well, let us continue our tour then."

He continued on, forcing her to snatch her skirts and hasten to catch up. Why did he shake his head? Did he not like something he saw? Was it something she said? She suppressed a sigh. How she wished she understood the opposite sex.

How she wished she understood this man.

Chapter Six

They'd shared four evening meals exactly now. Well, five including this one but Grace did not include this one as they were only part way through the main course of partridges. How Mary cooked such meals on her own, Grace had yet to fathom but the woman clearly loved to cook. The last time she had eaten like this was when her father was alive.

Every time she arrived for dinner, she was tempted to seat herself all the way at the end of the long table. The polished wood gleamed, set with a single candelabra and slightly rustic cutlery.

She had placed herself to Nash's right every one of those five nights. Eating practically miles away from one another would be ridiculous and she was yet to ask many of her hundreds of questions. But now she had paper and a pencil, and she had already noted several of her questions.

She glanced at the notes she had spread surreptitiously in her lap. She'd been so excited when writing them that they were not particularly legible, and the meagre light made them hard to read but she could fathom a few of them. Tomorrow, she would write them out neater and keep them on her person in case there were more chances to ask him questions.

She squinted at the first. It was the one that was plaguing her the most, she supposed, but the one Nash seemed least inclined to answer. Who was he and how did he come to be here? She shook her head, shoved in a forkful of meat, and paused while considering the second question.

There was no delicate way to ask these questions. Or at least, she had a complete inability to be delicate.

Once she had finished her mouthful, she fixed him with her gaze, waiting.

Still waiting. He ate a full three forkfuls before noticing her gaze upon him.

"Yes?"

"Why are you involved in this?" she blurted out.

"In this?" He glanced around. "Dinner? Well, I am rather hungry and—"

"No, I mean the kidnapping." Grace wrinkled her nose. "My aunt said she had heard it called...The Kidnap Club?"

He chuckled. "I have heard it called that too though we do not think of it as anything official."

"Oh good."

"Good?"

"Well, if it were me, I would have come up with something much more interesting to call it."

He lowered his fork and leaned forward. "Like what?"

She pursed her lips. "The Capture Club, perhaps?"

"The Capture Club?" he repeated. "How is that better than The Kidnap Club?"

She let her shoulders drop. "I suppose it isn't. But I'm certain, given time, I could think of something much more appealing."

"We're not overly interested in being appealing, Grace," he pointed out. "It's not like we're vying for members."

"How many of you are there exactly?"

"Three main members. Then we have Mary." He ticked his fingers off. "Tommy who sneaks in the fuel and food. We also have Hamper who aids with travel when needed and Mrs. Richmond when needed."

"And they all have specific roles?"

"Well, you met Russell. He's the kidnapper and escort I suppose. The others help out when needed."

"And the third?"

His brows lifted. "Your aunt did not tell you of him?"

She shook her head.

"Guy is the leader of this all. He put it together."

"But why?" She tilted her head. "That is what puzzles me the most. Is it for coin? Because surely risking death or the wrath of husbands or a potential duel isn't worth whatever you earn?"

Nash leaned back in his chair and laced his hands behind his head. "You would have to ask Guy why he continues down this path. Same with Russell. For me, it's an interesting way to pass time and, as you can see, I can do with the coin." He gestured around the dining room.

"Your family must have some wealth." She eyed the dusty portrait hanging over the fireplace. The man in it looked like an older version of Nash and from his clothing, it could only have been painted some thirty years ago. Had that been Nash's father? Had he passed away and left him without a penny? Perhaps that was why he avoided talking of it. She had been young when she lost her father, but she still remembered the pain.

She slid a hand across the table, leaving it near his fingers. "You can cry if you wish."

"Cry?"

"That is your father, is it not?" She nodded to the portrait.

He stiffened and she saw the muscles in his jaw work. "It is."

"I lost my father when I was eight. I cried for a long time. Sometimes, I still have moments when I miss him painfully."

Nash shook his head vigorously. "I do not miss my father."

"I see."

He picked up his fork and stabbed the meat forcefully. "You see nothing, Grace. There is nothing of which to talk."

"I see."

"Damn it, stop saying that."

The words burned on her tongue, so she took a bite of dinner to mask them. She did see though. See that there was a lot of pain where his father was concerned. Had he been a horrible man perhaps? It was so hard to tell with Nash. He was all charm and wit, but the substance remained hidden. Gosh, how she wished she could scrawl some notes quickly. Usually, she liked to study animals, but Nash was as fascinating as any creature she'd ever seen.

HE SHOULDN'T HAVE snapped but at least now her questions would cease. He didn't consider himself to have many secrets but good Lord, he was tired of thinking about his father and his betrayal.

A few moments of blessed silence passed. He finished his dinner and dabbed his mouth with the napkin. Grace glanced at her lap several times and a crease appeared between her brow.

Had her napkin slid off her lap perhaps? Maybe she had spilled something and was embarrassed.

"I know we are dining in a grand house—or what was once a grand house—but you do not need to feel as though you must behave formally," he assured her. "You are going to be here for some time, and I'd like it if we could be friends."

"Formal?" she repeated. "Friends?"

"Yes, you seem a little uncomfortable."

Her gaze shot up from her lap and she shook her head. "No."

"No to being friends or no to being uncomfortable?"

"I will admit this is strange to me, but I am not uncomfortable." She lifted her shoulders as though she had just taken in a deep breath. "I don't really have friends so I suppose...that would be nice."

With any other woman, he would have thought this as some false modesty or a way of trying to draw compliments from him. However, he didn't think she had a false bone in her body.

"You must have a best friend at least. Every girl has a best friend."

"Not me. Unless you count my aunt." She paused. "That sounds rather depressing, though my aunt is lovely indeed."

Her expression brightened at the mention of the aunt. It was about the first time he'd seen her smile. If it could be counted as a smile. The slight curve of delicate lips would certainly put the Mona Lisa to shame in its allusivity.

"Your aunt raised you?"

"Since I was eight," she confirmed. The smile broadened slightly. "She is the kindest woman in the world."

"She sounds wonderful."

"I miss her," she admitted. "We have hardly spent a day apart since I came to her."

"Does she not like you spending time with other people?"

"Oh goodness, she would love it if I could make friends, but my uncle...well, let us just say he makes life difficult and I am not practiced in making friends."

"Your uncle is the one forcing the wedding, is he not?"

"Yes," she said tightly.

"You can say it you know." He leaned forward, searching her gaze. He saw it when she'd muttered his name. So much anger there and yet she was holding back.

"Say what?"

"Whatever it is you are feeling about him."

She pressed her lips together. "I cannot."

"Why?"

"Because...because saying things as a woman is dangerous. We cannot speak out."

"You can speak out here. You are entirely safe."

She cast a glance about the room as though there were spies in every corner, just waiting to hear whatever it was that was going on in her head. She opened her mouth then closed it.

"Say it," he urged.

"Well, I...I..." She lifted her chin. "I hate him."

He grinned at the vehemence behind the words.

"I hate him," she repeated more aggressively. "He is vain and stupid and greedy. He...he's a big, ugly old lummox."

"Good, good."

"And I hate his room. With his ugly red chair. And all the dark wood. And those horrible red curtains. I hate him and I hate his room."

Nash chuckled, enjoying the way her eyes sparked and how her cheeks bloomed with color far too much.

"I hate how he treats my aunt. Oh Lord, I hate it so much." She dropped her face to her hands and several heartbeats of silence passed before she lifted her face. "I think I might need that cry now."

Nash practically jumped from his seat to come to her aid. He slipped into the chair beside her and wrapped an arm about her shoulders. She dropped her head to his chest so hard he feared she had done some damage to both of them, but the pain passed as he rubbed her shoulders while her tiny body jerked, and she smothered little sniffles against his chest.

He eyed the top of her head and forced himself to breathe through his mouth. Her hair smelled of soap. No different to the scent he smelled every time he took a bath. But that clean, fresh scent made him feel lightheaded from some inane reason. As did the feel of her body against his.

Touch her.

He was touching her, damn it. He had her shoulder grasped firmly in one hand. And, look, now he was wrapping another arm about her. That was quite enough touching.

Touch her more.

Hell's teeth. He swallowed hard. How easy it would be to sweep a hand along her chin, raise her face to his, and drop a gentle kiss on that tiny, cupid bow mouth.

How easy and stupid it would be. He'd never kissed a woman in his care, and he would not start now. What a cad he had to be to consider kissing a crying, vulnerable woman. He glanced at his father's portrait as it peered down disapprovingly at him. The last thing he wanted to do was prove his father right. He would not kiss her—not now, not ever.

"Dessert is here," trilled Mary. "We have trifle, baked apples, and Banbury cakes. I will admit, I got a little carried away." He heard her footsteps still. "Oh."

Nash twisted to view her. "It is fine," he murmured. "She is just having a little cry."

Grace straightened and swiped hands across her face. "I am fine now, thank you." She smiled at Mary. "Dessert looks delicious."

He frowned as she broke contact. She did indeed look fine. "Are you certain you are well?" he pressed.

"Oh yes," she said, taking a generous helping of trifle. "A cry is good for your health. My father always said as much." She delved into the dessert with relish. "Thank you," she said through a mouthful. "You were right. I needed that."

Nonplussed, Nash watched her finish a pile of trifle then move on to the next dessert. He had to wonder where on earth she put it all. Someone her size, he'd have expected to eat like a sparrow but instead she ate like a hawk. This was no ordinary woman.

Chapter Seven

Wind and rain beat at the windowpane. Nash grunted and rolled over in his bed. Another blast of wind struck the building and he sat up. The weather wasn't likely to improve anytime soon, so it was doubtful he'd be getting to sleep anytime soon either.

He rubbed a hand over his face, fumbled for the tinder box, and lit a candle. He stepped onto the cold wood floor and shuddered then snatched up his robe from the nearby chair, shoving his fists blindly into the arms and cinching it tight. If he couldn't sleep, he doubted Grace could either.

He should check on her.

But she would have come to him had she needed him, surely?

No, perhaps not. It was hard to tell with her. She was the sort of woman who never asked for anything. Never seemed to need anything. He frowned to himself. It made her difficult but not in that usual haughty sort of way. At least with most women, one could fling something nice their way and they would be beaming at him and thanking him ever so much. With Grace, he had yet to figure out quite what she wanted in life and, for some damned reason, he really, really wanted to give her a reason to smile.

However, if she desperately needed something, she would come to him. Right?

God knows, she was about the most honest, blunt woman he'd ever met. If the gale outside scared her, she would not hesitate to come to him.

Maybe.

Blowing out a breath, he pressed his face to the window. A cloak of darkness surrounded the house, offering him nothing but a few splatters of rain on the window and not even the outline of a tree or two. No way to tell when the storm might pass.

He grabbed the candle and eased open the door, peering up and down the darkened corridor. Wind whistled through a crack somewhere in the building but there was no hesitant woman outside his door, seeking comfort.

Of course there wasn't. She was just fine.

He should still make certain, though. After all, her welfare was his responsibility.

Nash closed his bedroom door behind him, ensuring to do so gently. Perhaps she was one of those unusual people who could sleep through gales like this. If she was, he envied her indeed.

Pausing outside her bedroom, he listened for a moment. The faint sound of the wind howling made him freeze. Good lord, it sounded awful coming from her room. One of the windows might be slightly ajar or perhaps broken. He'd have to move her as there was no chance he could get it fixed anytime soon.

He scowled. That really was quite the racket. Surely she wasn't sleeping through that? A pang of guilt thread through him. From what he could tell, she'd lived a basic sort of a life with her uncle. What a shame he had no funds to ensure she at least enjoyed living in luxury here. Unfortunately, as long as he was cut off from his father, he had nothing to spare to maintain the house any better than it already was.

As had been promised, he thought bitterly.

He rapped a knuckle on the door and waited a few moments.

Definitely asleep then.

He should just leave her.

He twisted around then turned back. Hand to the doorknob, he rotated it slowly and slipped inside.

The warm glow of the room made him blink. Coals still glowed in the fireplace and several candles and an oil lamp were lit about the room. His gaze fell on the bed, but it was empty, the blankets tossed aside. He slowly shut the door behind him and placed the candle on the armoire.

Where was she? Clearly, she had been here only moments ago, and it was careless of her indeed to leave everything lit unless she was only gone for a moment.

He scanned the room again as though he might have missed the petite woman curled up in a corner somewhere. On the small table near the fireplace, sheets of paper were stacked carefully, and he stepped over to them, spreading them with his fingers.

His gaze fell to his name.

Was she writing about him?

A howl of wind echoed through the room. He whirled at the sound and frowned. That was no howling wind, that was...

No, it couldn't be.

He listened again. It damn well was. It was Grace. She was in the adjoining dressing room.

And she was singing.

Well, if it could be called singing. There was certainly some resemblance of a tune but not one he recognized and the sounds she was making were more sort of squawks. They reminded him a little of when he'd visited Lord Kirkland when he was a child and had spent far too long teasing his talking parrot.

Who would have thought such a delicate woman could make such a racket?

The singing continued then stopped. Footsteps padded across the floor and Nash's heart came to a halt. She was coming back into the room.

And she would find him here. In his robe. Nosing through her belongings.

He wasn't sure it was the cleverest move, but it was the only option open to him. He darted down by the side of her bed.

So there he was, cowering in her room, ducked by her bed like some awful intruder while she moved about the bedroom, humming to herself. He grimaced. What a foolish thing to do. He should have remained where he was and explained he had simply been checking on her.

But, no, he had to follow his stupid instincts and lurk like some sort of...lurking thing, and if she discovered him, he'd give her the fright of her life.

Perhaps he could slip out once she had gone back to bed. Maybe she wouldn't notice there was someone skulking about her bedroom.

Her humming increased in pitch and he winced. The woman couldn't even hold a tune in a hum.

He peered over the blankets and his heart hammered to a stop.

God Lord, now he was not just some sort of skulking creature, he was also a pervert.

The candlelight silhouetted her against the thin sheath of her slip. Silhouetted every little bit of her body. He could make out her tiny, tiny waist and his fingers itched to span it. There was a slight rise of breasts too.

Pervert. Definitely a pervert. He should look away or cough loudly—quickly before he saw anything else.

She turned and he groaned inwardly. Now he saw the curve of her rear.

Stupid Nash. He should have just stayed in bed and trusted she would come to him if she needed anything. Cleary, she was utterly content, singing to herself in that tiny, thin sheath of fabric, all nearly naked and far too—

It was no good.

He rose sharply. "Grace—"

She screamed, whirled, and flung herself across the bed at him.

AS HER FIST landed square in the intruder's gut, she flopped onto the bed. Grace scrabbled backward off the bed, fists raised.

"Oh no."

It only took her a moment to figure out the intruder was not some stranger or, indeed, an intruder at all.

"Nash!"

Shoving her hair from her face, she dashed around the bed to put a hand to his shoulder. Doubled over, he wheezed in a few breaths and Grace grimaced.

"I thought you were an intruder," she explained.

"I know," he muttered, an arm banded about his waist. He finally straightened and her gaze fell to his open robe. And underneath that, his open shirt. Held together by a mere thread, looped loosely into a bow, she saw all the way down to his naval. Her cheeks heated.

"I'm so sorry." She touched his shoulder again and snapped her hand back swiftly when her traitorous gaze fell onto his chest once more. She'd seen men's chests before. In drawings or on statues, of course, but still it should have been enough to prevent her from reacting this way to a mere bit of flesh. After all, that's all it was. Skin over sinew and muscle.

Lots of muscle. So much muscle. She cocked her head. How was it he was so strong? How did he get those bumps on his abdomen? She glanced up to find him looking at her with a raised eyebrow.

"Are you hurt?" she asked hastily.

He shook his head and leaned a casual arm on the poster of the bed. "Not at all."

She eyed him. "It seemed like I hurt you very much." She glanced at her fist. "I didn't know I could punch."

"You took me by surprise that's all."

"I'm sorry I hurt you. But you took me by surprise too."

"You did not hurt me," he insisted.

"I must have more strength than I realized." She bunched her hand into a fist and tried to recall how she had thrown that punch in the first place. "How fascinating."

"You did not hurt me," he said through gritted teeth.

"Maybe I shall see if I can punch something else."

"No!" He held up his hands.

"Oh no, I won't hurt you again, I promise."

"You did not hurt me," he repeated.

"Maybe I should punch some pillows." She dropped her hand and eyed him. "What are you doing here anyway?"

"I came to check if you were well, what with the gale and all that." He indicated outside.

"Oh." For the first time since she'd struck him, she recalled she was still in her chemise. Practically naked really. She reached for the blanket on the bed and Nash's gaze shot up to the ceiling. Oh Lord, she had probably given him a finer view down her shift than she'd had of his chest.

That she still had.

Snatching up the blanket, she held it against her front. No doubt a man like Nash had seen many a woman naked and most of them likely had a lot more to offer than she did. Nannette Arbuckle had always reminded her how much she looked like a boy. She supposed Nash was probably shocked to see such an unfeminine body.

"The wind..." he muttered, finally returning his gaze to hers. "It's quite aggressive tonight."

She lifted a shoulder. "It doesn't bother me. We are in quite a solid building, but I shall admit the noise on the windows was keeping me awake."

"I...uh...heard you singing."

"Oh dear."

"I thought it was the wind at first then I realized..."

"Did I wake you?" She clapped a hand to the side of her face whilst keeping the blanket firmly in the other. "I am sorry. First, I wake you, then I hurt you."

"You did not hurt me."

"I am quite well I promise, and I shan't sing anymore. You can go back to bed."

"So long as you are quite well."

"Yes, yes, I am quite well." She paused and scowled. "Though, why were you hiding behind my bed?"

Nash stilled. "I was just, uh, well that is..." He lifted a shoulder. "I thought I saw something."

"Something?"

"Yes, but it was nothing."

"I see."

His gaze darted briefly over her then he started to shuffle sideways away from her bed. He came around the end of it, paused in front of her, and reached out. Her heart stilled. She could hear her breaths in her ears. His hand moved at the most infinitesimal pace. He plucked the shoulder of her shift and hauled it higher, covering a bare shoulder she had not even realized was exposed.

Grace tried to swallow the knot gathering in her throat and failed. Why did the room feel so unbearably warm? Why was he standing in front of her? Why could she not resist staring at his chest?

"Well, goodnight," he said formally, his hand still upon her shoulder.

"Yes, goodnight."

"My bedroom is...that is..." He coughed. "I am only down there if you need me."

"I know."

"Yes, of course you do."

His hand had to have left singe marks by now, surely? She glanced at her shoulder, expecting to see steam rising from where his fingers were splayed.

He jolted and snatched his hand back. "Goodnight then."

"Goodnight."

Nash backed away and stumbled over where Claude was curled up on a blanket. The cat opened an eye, gave a yawn, then closed it again, unperturbed by the disturbance.

"Sorry," he muttered then hurried out of the door, slamming it shut behind him with such a bang that Claude jerked fully awake.

After a few moments of staring at the closed door, she sank onto the bed. Even if it were not windy outside, she doubted she'd sleep now. How strange that moment had been. Why had Nash been so odd? Why had he touched her for so long?

She spread her fingers over where his hand had lingered, still able to feel his touch. She knew human touch was important—that children who were embraced more often tended to be more well-rounded humans. But she'd never heard of a simple touch making one feel like one was on fire. All over too. Every part of her was aflame, tingling with some strange sensation that pooled low in her stomach. It compounded, too, when she considered what she had seen of him tonight.

Claude jumped onto the bed and butted his head against her hand. She sighed and stroked her hand down Claude's patchy fur. "Men are strange creatures," she said to the cat.

And intriguing. Or at least Nash was. Intriguing indeed.

Chapter Eight

"Grace said she hurt you yesterday."

Nash made a dismissive noise and ducked his head behind the week-old newspaper, away from Mary's inquisitive gaze. Although they could not obey the usual formalities in their unusual circumstances, Nash hardly needed Mary knowing he was in her bedroom last night.

Though it sounded like Grace had already told her. He sighed, folded the paper, and set it on the dining table. "When are we going to get a new newspaper? I've read this one five times already, and if I have to read about Lady P's feathers one more time, I might very well shoot myself for mere entertainment value."

Mary shook her head and took the newspaper off him, tucking it under one arm while she tidied away the plates from breakfast. "You are not normally so uptight. She really must have hurt you."

"She did not hurt me, no matter what she says."

"She felt quite awful about punching you."

"Have you seen her, Mary? There are five-year-old girls with more strength than her." He jabbed a finger at the table. "She did. not. hurt. me," he insisted.

She lifted a shoulder and paused by the window. "At least the weather has cleared now. Grace is outside with the cat."

"Damned ugly creature," Nash muttered.

"You really are quite grumpy today. Are you certain she did not hurt you?" Mary turned away from the window and leaned against the sill, plates in hand. "What were you doing in her room anyway? You know the earl will have your head if there is anything untoward happening."

He cocked his head. "You must think me a fool."

"No, not at all." Her lips curved. "Well, you do have a history of making foolish mistakes, everyone knows that, but I've never known you to touch one of the women."

"And I still will not. I was simply doing my duty and ensuring she was well. In case you had not noticed, we had quite a storm here last night."

Mary nodded. "I did notice. One of the trees is down along the lane. My brothers are going to chop it up later and I'll send Tommy along with some of the wood tomorrow."

"And a new newspaper, please."

"Yes, yes." She straightened and peered out of the window. "She's quite pretty you know."

Nash regretted giving away the newspaper now. He should have kept it and continued to pretend to read it. Then he wouldn't have to deal with Mary's pervasive stare. "Who is?"

"Grace, of course."

He shrugged. "I don't think she is. Too small."

Mary shook her head vigorously. "She has a pretty face. I'd wager there would be many a man intrigued by her, especially given how small she is. Makes them want to be all primitive and protect her."

"I am protecting her because I'm being paid to do it. And quite handsomely too. Not because she is small or vaguely pretty."

And he didn't want to think of other men wishing to protect her.

"I thought you said she wasn't pretty."

He paused. "Well, you said she was. I was only copying your words."

Her smile widened. "You're allowed to find her pretty, Nash. Lord knows, you don't normally watch your tongue when it comes to the attractiveness of our guests."

"A man can change."

He pushed back the chair and rose. He was rather over being quizzed as to whether he found Grace pretty or not. Did it matter? Did he have to defend himself simply because he couldn't get the image of her silhouette out of his mind? Because he'd spent the entire night picturing what it might have been like to drag her down onto the bed, slide up her shift, and have a taste of those little rosebuds he'd stolen a peek at?

Good God, he should have remained seated.

He drew in a long breath and strode over to the window. He didn't want to look at her, really he didn't, but he could not face Mary in his current predicament.

Sure enough, Grace was outside, seated on a stone bench with Claude curled upon her lap. She had a book in one hand, and another curled protectively about the cat. She wore the same gown she'd arrived in, a cream affair with lines of blue sewn through it and a high neckline. Her cape was pulled tight about her and her hair was pinned neatly to her head in her usual no-nonsense manner.

Nothing about the image could make his situation any worse, but of course it did.

He grimaced to himself and continued to draw breaths through his nostrils. *Think of all the money you would lose if you compromised her.*

Ridiculous, he wasn't going to compromise her. He'd resisted bigger temptations than some small, odd woman who rescued ugly cats and was probably going to read through his whole library before the end of her stay.

"I won't be here for dinner tonight," Mary reminded him, "so there's a cold platter in the kitchen."

"Yes," he murmured.

"Any word from Russell on the ransom?"

Nash shook his head and rubbed a hand across his face. This whole situation had him feeling prickly. They never normally did ransoms, but not only did they want the money, it would help delay matters and prevent anyone searching for her. They had sent out a threatening note or even a demand before but never collected on it.

The chances of anyone finding Grace here were ridiculously slim anyway. No one would expect the heir to a viscountcy to be involved in kidnapping and Guildham estate was all but forgotten about. There was a reason they trusted few to help them too.

"Well, only three weeks more and Grace can return home an heiress," Mary said brightly. "I bet she shall have many charming men at her door once that happens."

Nash merely grunted. Grace had only spoken of setting up a home with her aunt but what woman wasn't swayed by a charming, handsome man? He imagined Mary was right and she'd be snapped up swiftly once word of her inheritance got out—even if she had been kidnapped and potentially 'ruined'. After all, what was a little ruination when it came to a pretty woman with a nice bit of wealth behind her.

Damn it.

Mary was right. She was pretty. Too pretty. And he hated the thought of her marrying some cad who wouldn't understand her one jot just for her money. He'd have to counsel her perhaps. Ensure she remained wary.

He snorted to himself. Who was he to give advice?

"Are you certain you can't remain for the day?" he asked Mary, finally able to turn and face her.

"Sorry, I have too much work to do at home." She picked up the last plate. "You are not scared she might hurt you again, are you?"

He clenched his jaw. "She didn't hurt me!"

Mary laughed and left the room before he could say anything else. Damn that woman. Damn Grace. Damn them all.

GRACE TURNED HER face up to the sun. Or what there was of it. The storm had passed, leaving the air fresh and scented like wet grass. The sun attempted to press through the clouds at regular intervals and Grace inhaled deeply.

Her father always insisted on the health benefits of being outside, even sometimes without a parasol or bonnet. She understood why now. Although she tended to prefer being indoors, after a night like last night, she felt the need to be sitting in the breeze, letting the sun touch her face.

Claude stirred, did a little rotation on her lap, then settled again. Grace closed the book she had been reading and set it on the bench beside her then turned her attention to the cat. She smoothed her hand over his ears and head then followed the curl of his body. He purred loudly, the sound vibrating through to her legs.

"At least you are content, Claude," she murmured.

Though, what had she expected from this whole venture? If she was honest, she had barely thought it through when her aunt had suggested the idea—unusual for her indeed. She thought everything through, even down to how many eggs she should have for breakfast. But desperation had made her careless and she had eagerly agreed to this kidnapping.

Anything to get away from the awful Mr. Worthington.

She wrinkled her nose. Perhaps that was why she was so intrigued by Nash. She could not claim they were overly acquainted as yet, but he was entirely different to Mr. Worthington. He was charming, yes, but there was no sense of falseness behind it. It was just who Nash was. He moved and breathed and lived charm.

The fact he had come to check on her last night made her feel a little soft inside too, somehow. He'd been concerned for her welfare. Maybe it was because he was being paid to do so but she liked it anyway. The only other people who had ever cared for her welfare were her aunt and father, and, of course, they were obliged to.

"Nash is obliged to as well," she told the cat.

Claude nudged her hand, reminding her she was not doing a good enough job of petting him.

"You are right," Grace said. "I am being far too distracted and silly. Who cares if he is nice to me? There are plenty of nice people in the world." She pursed her lips. "I think, anyway."

"I'll see you tomorrow, Grace," Mary called from the track that led away from the house, giving her a quick wave.

Grace waved back, ignoring the little twist in her stomach that reminded her she'd be alone with Nash all day and night. Mary had warned her as much and Grace had managed to react indifferent to it, but it excited her for some reason.

"That's silly too. We are alone every evening anyway." She watched Mary head away from the house and swallowed hard. "And we shall be alone for many more days until I turn one-and-twenty, shan't I, Claude? In which case I must begin behaving sensibly."

"Have you ever behaved anything other than sensibly?"

Grace leapt up from the bench, disturbing Claude, who flew off her lap and dashed along the path toward the lawns. "Oh no." She darted after him and Nash followed, swiftly taking over her and scooping up the cat.

Claude squirmed in his hold and tried to swipe at him. Nash jerked back his head and narrowly avoided spread claws. Grace quickly took the cat off him and murmured some soothing words until Claude begrudgingly gave up his wriggling.

"I'm sorry," she said breathlessly. "I was silly to take him outside so soon."

"Is that what you were scolding yourself for?"

"Yes. No. Um..." She released a long breath. She could hardly admit she had been scolding herself for spending too much time thinking of him.

"Shall we take Claude inside before he makes another attempt at escape?" He glanced up at the sky. "And before the weather breaks."

She nodded, glancing up at the gray clouds that had gathered, and followed him into the hallway. Once the door was shut, she placed the cat on the floor. He sauntered over to a threadbare chaise in the corner and swiftly settled.

Nash grinned. "His little adventure has worn him out already."

Grace struggled to reply. She'd glanced at him and found herself captivated by the flash of white teeth and the crinkles around his eyes. Now she wanted to go and write more about him but that was probably silly too. It would not help with how much room he took up in her brain.

"I missed you at breakfast this morning," he said after several heartbeats of silence.

She nodded. "I wanted to make the most of the nice weather, b-before it changed."

"You can walk around the estate if you wish but stay within sight of the house. If you are spotted, then—"

"Yes." He had given her very few rules to live by but the primary one was *do not let anyone see you*. She didn't think that would be a problem. Exploring was not really her thing unless one counted digging through the library.

"I think I have had enough fresh air for now anyway. I might go and find another book to read." She paused and pressed a hand to her mouth. "The book! I left it outside in the rain."

"Not to fear, I'll go and rescue it." He headed outside before she could protest and returned swiftly, his hair damp and thickly curled. He offered her the book. "Grace?" he prompted when she remained frozen in place.

She felt her mouth ajar but could do nothing to persuade herself to shut it. A raindrop trickled down his chin and she followed the path of it, down his neck to where his shirt was slightly open. Would it travel all the way down or soak into his clothing? Would it go past those bumps on his stomach?

Maybe lower.

A strange squeak escaped her before she could prevent it and she snatched the book from him, muttering a quick thank you and dashing up the stairs.

"I thought you wanted the library," she heard him call but she ignored him and hastened into her bedroom.

She slammed the door shut and pressed her back to it, the book clutched to her throbbing chest. These thoughts made no sense. None whatsoever. She was a well brought up lady who cared little for outward appearances and more about what was occurring in someone's mind. She most certainly should not be considering what was down...down...

Oh God. She clapped a hand to her face. This was more than silly, this was nonsensical, this was addled. A girl like her had no business thinking about a man like Nash.

No business at all.

Chapter Nine

Nash never usually welcomed the arrival of Russell at the estate.

It meant something was wrong.

Today, however, he rose from his chair in the drawing room with a grin and greeted him with a hearty handshake.

Russell either didn't notice Nash's relief at seeing him or didn't care. The tall chap swept a hand through chestnut hair and dropped his hat onto a nearby table. "How's the girl?"

Fascinating? No, that wouldn't do. Too pretty? Couldn't say that either. "Fine," he said instead.

"Good, good."

Russell paced past the window that looked out over the overgrown lawns. His long legs covered the distance in a few paces, so he twisted when he reached the wall and turned to repeat the movement.

"I take it things are not 'fine' on your end?" Nash rested an elbow on the mantelpiece, adopting a pose far more casual than he felt. The past week had left him tangled in a knot, his gut constantly bunched with...well, everything.

Desire, intrigue, more desire.

He was losing the plot.

Hence, him welcoming the intrusion. At least, momentarily. If things were not going to plan, it could put Grace in some sort of danger and that made his far-too-sensitive gut tighten yet again. He couldn't let anything happen to her.

"Where is the girl anyway?" Russell asked.

"In the library. Probably with the cat."

Russell made a face. "That thing hardly counts for a cat."

Nash shrugged. "It's not so bad."

"I didn't even think you liked cats." He narrowed his gaze at Nash.

He shrugged again. "They clean themselves and are quite good at keeping one warm."

Good Lord, now he sounded like Grace.

Nash shook his head but didn't comment on his sudden turn around on the subject of cats. "The uncle has requested proof that she is alive."

"Ah."

"It is a delay. Guy has heard he doesn't wish to pay the ransom and is sending out men to search for her instead."

"It's not the first time we have had people search for one of the women."

"No, but we have this fiancé on the case too, and he's known to associate with some unsavory types. They won't think twice about hurting people to get information."

"*Not* her fiancé," muttered Nash.

"Pardon?"

"Not her fiancé," he repeated. "She never accepted him."

Russell eyed him for a moment. "Well, the world thinks of him as that. It seems he is spreading quite the tale of how he misses his lovely bride and is willing to do anything to get her back."

"Apart from pay the ransom."

"Indeed."

"Bastard," he murmured under his breath, a fist curled at his side. Neither of those men cared for Grace. All they wanted was her inheritance. Hell fire, he'd like to take them both and—

"A lock of hair should do it."

Nash glanced up. "What?"

"We'll send a strand of hair along with a note from her, begging for them to pay the ransom and to stay away lest we harm her."

Nash blew out a breath. It wasn't the first time they had to make threats to draw out the kidnapping process and ensure the family didn't hunt the women but he didn't much like the thought of Grace writing to her non-fiancé, even if it was with artificial woe.

"They'll never find her here."

Russell nodded. "But it's better to play it safe. You still have nearly three weeks until her birthday."

"The longest we've ever held a woman."

"Precisely. Everything about this situation is different to usual. We must do all we can to keep her safe."

Different was about right. Nothing about Grace was the same as the other women. Not the way she looked or behaved or even ate or drank. She analyzed everything and constantly took notes. He still had a hankering to see what she was writing about him, but he'd not had a chance to steal a look.

Would it be good things? It was hard to tell. She stared at him sometimes as though he were some curious specimen. Every now and then she'd cock her head whilst they were conversing, and he could see her mind ticking over. His desire to figure out exactly what was going on behind those eyes was almost as much as his desire to catch her in her shift again.

"I'll get her to write the letter," Nash finally agreed.

"Don't forget the lock of hair."

"You want it now?"

"I do not plan to stay long. I have a way to travel and we need to get that letter delivered with haste," Russell explained.

Nash didn't argue. Russell never seemed to need rest or food or good conversation. The man moved about the country with the same sort of pace that his long legs crossed the drawing room. All that travelling would drive Nash insane, but Russell always enjoyed it, flitting from one place to the next. Russell had once said he'd never had roots so he couldn't understand why people wanted to stay in the same place all the time.

Nash, however, was quite content remaining at the estate. New kidnappees were always enough to keep him entertained.

Though *entertained* was the wrong word for it this time. He enjoyed Grace's odd brand of company to be certain, but she was also driving him out of his wits. The no-nonsense woman likely had no idea how captivating she was.

And no idea how damned pretty she was.

Even if he would never, ever, ever admit that to Mary or anyone else. He was a professional after all and he was not going to bloody well ruin his record of keeping his hands off the women now.

SHE HEARD HIS footsteps coming down the corridor, but Grace kept her attention on the book in her lap. She made the most of the fire in the library by sitting on the rug in front of it with a blanket on her lap. Claude had opted to join her too—not surprising considering the room was cold indeed. But it was safe here. The books kept her mind from wandering too much.

Most of the time anyway.

The words jumbled in front of her eyes and she frowned, forcing herself to concentrate. Her heart leaped when the door to the library opened and she very nearly leapt with it, but she forced her body to remain stiff, her chin lowered, while she kept up the pretense of reading.

The last thing she needed was to seem like some lovesick girl, eager to jump to her feet because of Nash's mere presence. *Not* that she was lovesick.

However, her rather foolish preoccupation with thinking of him could make it seem that way. Flirtations and swooning over men was not for her—it never had been. She didn't understand the opposite sex, nor did she wish to. The only man who had ever been kind to her was her father. She had a suspicion that good men were few and far between.

Her gaze flicked to the slip of paper she was using as a bookmark. But, of course, she was lying to herself. She wanted to understand Nash, and the bookmark proved it. She'd been using it to make notes on his turns of phrases or the little bits of information he let slip. He was heir to a title so presumably wealthy, yet he lived in this draughty, worn house in the middle of nowhere. He was most certainly not married, that much she had garnered. Mary had intimated there was some sort of falling out in the family and that explained his lack of available money but that he never talked of it.

She wished he would talk to her of it. How she longed to understand him.

He cleared his throat and she looked up, sweeping her gaze over the long length of him and catching herself nearly sighing over the perfect fit of his waistcoat and jacket.

Sighing over men was ridiculous. She'd seen girls do it from a young age even when the boys did not deserve it. It only left them looking like fools.

And, Lord knows, she'd look a huge fool to swoon and sigh over Nash. The man was remarkably handsome and extremely charming. Certainly not the sort to be interested in a woman like her with little understanding of social niceties and a body like a boy.

"You two look cozy there."

"It's the warmest place in the house." She spied furrows between his brows. "What is the matter?"

"As yet, our ransom is unpaid."

She closed her eyes briefly. "I am not surprised, though I had rather hoped my uncle would show some care for my welfare, even if it was simply to get me back to marry Mr. W." She set aside the book and eased an annoyed Claude off her lap before standing. "Though surely the later he pays, the better. If he pays, I would have to return."

He shook his head. "If we ever ask for ransom, we never usually take it. It is usually just a delaying tactic. We'd send another letter, claiming he had someone watching or had gone for aid. Anything to delay a hunt for you."

"So how is it a problem that he has not paid?"

"He has people out looking for you."

A wash of cold spread through her, pooling in her stomach. "He will not find me," she said, the statement more of a question than she wanted it to be.

"He will not," he said firmly. "I will make sure of that, Grace, I promise you."

She pressed hands to her stomach. "I only need a little while longer and then he can no longer make use of me."

Nash took her arms in his hands, forcing her to look at him. "We will send another letter. Russell is here to ensure it is delivered. We will have you write one, begging him to ensure your safety by calling off any searches."

"I suppose that might work."

"It will if he thinks we will harm you."

"Very well, I will write one straight away."

"Russell suggested we do something else too."

"Oh?"

He touched a loose strand of hair by her face, making the hairs on her arms stand on end underneath her sleeves. "A lock of hair. Proof we have you."

"My hair?"

"Yes." He tugged a penknife out of a jacket pocket and flicked it open. She jumped at the sudden movement. He smiled. "I'll be gentle, I promise."

Grace put a hand to her hair. "I am not vain but, well, I do not have many other attributes and I do like my hair."

His smile widened. "Grace, you have many, many attributes, and one lock of hair will not take away from that."

She eased out a breath and nodded. Drawing out all the pins and fisting them in one hand, she shook her hair loose with the other. "Perhaps from underneath," she suggested, "then it will not show."

"Good idea."

Nash moved behind her. His fingers in her hair made her want to jolt again so she kept her muscles stiff, barely breathing in case she gave herself away.

She enjoyed him touching her far too much.

He swept aside her hair and his fingers brushed the nape of her neck. She closed her eyes and concentrated on her stifled breaths. In...out...in...was it her imagination or could she feel his breath upon her neck? In...out...Good God, how long did it take for him to cut a lock of hair?

"Are you done?"

His fingers jerked away from her neck and her hair fell back into place. She turned to find him holding a small lock of her hair. Brow creased, looking slightly dazed, he gave a cough. "All done," he announced. "I'll take this to Russell right away."

"Oh, the letter—"

Gone. Vanished. With a few steps, he left the room before she could suggest she write the letter now. She eyed the spot where she'd seen him last. She held her breath and waited for him to return when he realized she had not yet written the note.

But he didn't return.

"Silly," she muttered to herself. Why did she want him to come back? So she could see that odd expression of his again and try to fathom what it was in aid of? Or so he could touch her once more? She shivered and pressed fingers to the back of her neck.

"Silly, silly, silly."

Grace returned to the fire and sank onto the blanket, depositing the hair pins on the nearby table. Claude ignored the little pat of invitation she gave and remained curled as close to the fire as possible. Plucking up her book, she opened it at her scribbled notes and tugged the pencil from behind her ear. She would write the letter in a minute. First she needed to write of *him*. At this point, she wasn't certain how useful noting her observations would be, but it was all she could do to get him from her mind.

Where he most certainly, absolutely did not belong.

Chapter Ten

Nash peered over the top of his three-day-old newspaper, turning his attention away from the advertisement on some annual winter sale he'd forgone the first few times of reading it. Now he was stuck reading the dregs because the lad who delivered the food hadn't been since Thursday. If he dared to fetch one himself, someone would likely recognize him and then word would get around that the house was occupied once more.

He wouldn't put Grace in that sort of danger, even for an up-to-date newspaper.

He waited for her to come past the door again. Why she lingered outside he did not know. Somehow, the drawing room had become somewhat his territory whilst the library had become hers. At dinner and most breakfasts, they joined together and conversed about many matters, Grace usually bluntly educating him on anything from the mating habits of snails to the history of the writing instrument. The woman was a damned walking encyclopedia.

And he liked it too much.

Therefore, it was much easier to remain away from her at all times, lest he throw himself at her feet and beg her to marvel him with her giant brain some more. He had friends of his who decried the idea that a woman might be so bold as to *think* became extremely unattractive, but Grace was the ultimate disproval of that hypothesis. Every time she opened her mouth, he grew more attracted to her.

He snorted to himself. *Hypothesis.* Now he was even sounding like her.

She flitted past the door again. He waited a few moments and she repeated the movement.

"Grace?" he called.

He heard a huff, soft footsteps, and then she appeared back in the doorway. Fingers curled around the doorframe, she peeked her head in. "Yes?"

"Did you want something?"

"No." She moved back, out of his sight, then reappeared. "Yes." She frowned. "No."

"Well, which is it?"

She stepped over the threshold and wound her hands together in front of her. "Is there word about the ransom yet? Or on my uncle's movements?"

Nash shook his head. "I will let you know as soon as there is."

"Good." She nodded briefly. "Excellent. Well, I shall..." She paused halfway through turning around. "Are you certain this will work?"

"The letter?"

"Yes. No." She waved a hand. "The whole thing. The kidnapping, the lock of hair, the hiding me away here. Will it work?"

"Grace, it will work," he assured her. "We've done this several times."

"But not with me."

"With other women. All of whom needed to escape."

"In different circumstances." She swiped a strand of hair from her face. "How can you be certain it will work this time? When things are different? One cannot perform the same action with different variables and expect the same results."

He folded his newspaper and rose from the chair to join her by the door. "Grace, what is this?"

"I have been thinking..." She blew out a breath. "I mean, perhaps I should go elsewhere. Go somewhere where no one knows I am there. I could go to an inn perhaps or...or..."

"There is no way in hell you are staying in some inn," he said firmly.

Her wide eyes clashed with his. "But I never really thought about it—the kidnapping thing that is. And I think about *everything*. One minute my aunt said we were going to have your help and the next I was being whisked away here. How do I even know it will work? How can I be certain my uncle won't find me and drag me home?"

"Because I won't let him."

She glanced at him up and down. "I do not doubt you have helped other women, but you underestimate my uncle and Mr. Worthington. You likely cannot think as they do. They are greedy men, willing to do anything to get my fortune."

"I know enough about needing a fortune." He gestured to the damp patch on the ceiling. "In case you had not noticed, I could do with some coin."

He knew about greed too really. That desperate need for money when one was running low. His father had accused him of being such a man, but he doubted telling Grace that would help matters.

"But you would never force someone to marry you simply for their money."

He gave a small smile. "I would rather hope I would not have to force them."

Grace made a frustrated sound. "This is why I cannot trust this. Or trust you. You are too quick to smile and make light of the situation."

His heart gave a painful jolt. She didn't trust him. Great.

"I told you I would protect you, Grace, and I damn well will."

"I think that perhaps my aunt was swayed by the man leading this venture. That perhaps she wasn't thinking straight." She closed her eyes briefly. "I was most certainly not. I should have thought of some other way of hiding for the month." She pressed fingers to her lips. "But I know my aunt would have been punished had I run away. I just know it."

"Your uncle sounds like a bastard," he muttered.

God, he wished she'd never had to live with the man. He wished he'd known her sooner. He could have intervened somehow. Protected her and her aunt from the cad and ensured she was never pressed into an engagement with this Worthington character.

But, of course, he wouldn't have noticed her had she not been placed directly in his path. Not someone without rank and wealth. The fact was, his circle had only involved the highest echelons of society and even after she had inherited her fortune, Grace would not be part of that.

"So you see why I must go. I cannot let him catch me."

"You are going nowhere."

"I saw your friend. I saw how agitated he was when he left. He walked briskly and with a straight spine."

Nash rolled his eyes. Of course Grace would analyze how Russell walked and jump to conclusions. "That's just how he walks."

"No, I know he was concerned."

Nash wasn't going to admit that most of the concern came from the fact Russell had seen how Nash had behaved after getting that blasted lock of hair from Grace. Simply touching her neck and resisting the urge to press a kiss to her soap-scented skin had him unravelling and Russell damn well knew it. The man had offered some short, sharp words of warning.

But he couldn't tell Grace that.

"Grace, I am sorry you do not trust me, but please believe me when I say this is the best place for you. Your aunt would have a fainting fit if she knew we had cast you off into some inn somewhere, and I wouldn't be able to live with myself."

"But it is the best way to ensure anonymity." She twined her hands tighter. "And I could keep moving, ensure no one catches up to me."

"No."

"My father always used to say if I was lost, I should stay in one place and he would find me. That is precisely why I should not stay here."

"No."

"IT MAKES SENSE for me to leave."

She had been thinking hard on the matter. There were too many people who knew she was here. Mary, of course, then the man her aunt talked to, and the delivery boy, not to mention the driver. If she simply fled on foot, no one could know where she had gone.

She should have just done that in the first place, just been brave and left. Now it was concluded she was kidnapped, her aunt would receive no recourse for her actions, and she could do as she wished. But for some silly reason, she felt she owed it to Nash to tell him of her plan.

"Do you really think you could survive out there on your own?"

"I know I am small, but I am not foolish. I could manage, I'm sure."

He shook his head vigorously. "You'd be eaten up in a second."

She kept her chin raised, too aware of how he towered over her, too conscious of the fine view of his neatly shaven jawline she had and how he smelled of warmth and fire smoke. How tempting it would be to fling herself at him and let him wrap his arms around her and protect her from a world so daunting. Except, she had little idea if he would even wish to do such a thing. So she was on her own.

"I have to try."

"You are safer here."

"How can you know?"

"You really think someone like you, out in the wide world of scoundrels and criminals, could survive for a moment alone?"

She wasn't certain but she had been thinking about it a lot. Any fate was better than being caught by her uncle and forced into marriage to Mr. Worthington. She lifted her shoulders. "I've survived this long under my uncle's hand."

"And for that I am sorry, but do not let that force you into foolish decisions."

"What would you even know about making decisions?" she cried. "You don't even have to decide what to eat every day. Mary does that for you."

"Damn it, Grace, I've made plenty of decisions in my time."

"Oh really?" She folded her arms. "I do not think you have ever had a moment of hardship. All you do is sit around all day and read newspapers and ride your horse and stroll around pretending to be a country gent."

His jaw worked. "So it comes to this, does it?" He narrowed his gaze at her. "You do not trust me and you have me marked as quite the useless sort of person."

"You cannot deny the evidence."

"Have you ever, for one moment, stopped and looked beyond evidence? Beyond what your eyes and your mind are telling you?"

"Of course not! Why would I?"

"Because sometimes you can get the measure of a man by listening to your heart," he snapped.

Grace blinked several times. His eyes were wild, his chest moving rapidly. She hadn't known Nash could get passionate about anything but, apparently, she had affected him somehow.

He would not sway her, though. She could not let him. He could beat his fists against his chest and talk of hearts over heads all he wished but she would not let a man dictate her movements to her, not ever again.

"I am going to leave."

"I will tie you up in your bedroom if you even try."

"You would not."

He took her wrist in his hand. "Do you want to test me?"

She inhaled a hot breath. "You cannot force me to do anything. I am done being forced, do you understand?"

"I can if it is in your best interests."

"No doubt my uncle fools himself into believing a marriage to Mr. Worthington is in my best interests. And I'm certain Mr. Worthington probably thought beating his wife was in her best interests too. As did he imagine pushing her down the stairs might teach her a lesson." Grace snatched her hand away from him. "I am utterly tired of men pretending they know what I need and what is best for me."

He opened his mouth then closed it and rubbed a hand over his jaw. "Grace, I—"

"I thought I was lying earlier. In saying that I did not trust you," she admitted. "But now you threaten to tie me up and hold me truly captive, I think I was correct. You are not to be trusted, Nash."

"Now that's not true—"

He reached for her and she ducked out of his way. "I'm going to my bedroom. You can barricade me in if you wish but I am still going to make plans to leave."

"I have no desire to do such a thing," he said softly.

"Good." She turned on her heel and marched out of the room then hastened upstairs.

Her eyes burned with the need to cry. She wasn't even certain why. She had made her decision—thought it through carefully even. Leaving and telling no one where she was going was the only logical thing to do.

And yet, the thought of leaving Nash made her heart hurt.

And *that* was most certainly not logical.

Chapter Eleven

He was a cad.

No.

An ass.

Nash shook his head. Worse than that.

An unfeeling bastard.

Of course he hadn't been able to understand Grace's fear. Of course he'd dismissed her desire to run. Told her she was a fool.

What did he know of forced marriages and men who would take advantage? He'd done nothing but sit around for the past four years, angry at his father for cutting him off. Oh yes, he'd partaken in The Kidnap Club, believing the noble cause would somehow make up for his hedonistic past but he'd done the bare minimum.

He blew out a breath and tugged the book from the library shelf. He hoped because of her tiny height she had yet to spot it and it would be a pleasant surprise. That was if she had not gathered all her belongings and escaped out of her bedroom window yet.

He couldn't let her go. He was right about that much. Out there on her own, she would be vulnerable, no matter how clever she was. There would be many a man or woman even who would take advantage of her, he feared.

That didn't mean he had to be such an ass about her fears, though.

No, unfeeling bastard, remember?

Cradling the book under his arm, he snatched up the plate of cold beef and clutched the bouquet of wildflowers in his other hand.

Today, he would do more than the bare minimum. He needed to understand exactly why Grace had agreed to the kidnapping. Not that he didn't know now. This fiancé sounded a piece of work and it took all Nash's willpower not to crush the delicate flower stems. Naïve, petite Grace would have no chance against such a man. He'd kill her eventually, for certain, especially once he got his hands on her money.

God damn, he'd like to take that man in a fair fight. Get him to throw a punch at someone his equal and see what happened. He knew nothing of the man, but he knew he could take him with ease. He was strong and fast but more than that, he would have the desire to protect Grace on his side.

But fighting was not going to fix this. No, right now, he needed to apologize to Grace and do what he arrogantly thought he was so good at—actually listen to her.

He made his way upstairs and tapped on the door. He hadn't expected an answer and he didn't get one. He tapped once more and leaned into the door, listening for movement. Christ, maybe she had gone out of the window. She had several blankets in there to fend off the cold. If one tied them together, one might be able to make a rope.

She had certainly not come downstairs—he'd put Mary to work guarding the hallway whilst he'd gathered his offerings.

He could wait no longer. Even if she was prancing around in her shift by candlelight, singing out of tune, he had to speak with her. Juggling the platter, the flowers, and the book, he eased down the door handle with an elbow and barged open the door with his shoulder.

Shit.

She was gone.

On the made bed, two dresses were splayed out. The fire remained lit and candles warmed the room. His heart pressed fiercely against his chest. He'd have to run after her, have to hunt her down. He could get Mary's brothers to help he supposed but they thought Mary worked for a nearby family. Or get Tommy—the lad who delivered the food—to assist him. He'd send word to Russell too. No one could evade Russell.

Even if it meant they'd have his head and he'd probably be kicked out of The Kidnap Club.

Damn, bugger, blast.

He shut the door behind him, and Claude darted out from behind the bed. He scowled. She wouldn't go anywhere without Claude.

And the window remained closed. No sign of ropes made of bedding either.

A little sniffle came from the other side of the bed. He let his shoulders sag and stepped around to find her on the floor, her back pressed against the bed frame, her knees pulled up to her chest, arms wrapped around them. She must have heard him, but she didn't look up.

"Grace," he said softly.

She kept her head bowed and made another snuffling noise.

He hated himself. He'd done this to her, made her cry. Was he not meant to be looking after her? Ensuring her every need, emotional and material, was met? What an utter failure he was.

He lowered himself to the floor, sliding in next to her and leaning back against the bed. "I am sorry."

Some time passed and he remained next to her, waiting. Eventually, she lifted her head a little and looked sideways at him. Even in the candlelight, he saw the redness in her eyes and the little damp tear tracks. His heart panged painfully.

Her brow furrowed. "What is that?" She nodded to his hands.

Nash gave an embarrassed shrug. "Offerings."

Her frown deepened.

He put the plate on the floor. "Cold beef for Claude." He glanced around for the cat who had yet to sniff out the meat. "Flowers for you." He held them out. "They were all I could find at this time of year, but I think they're quite pretty."

She peered at them as though he were offering her a giant bunch of squirming snakes. He held them out for a few moments more then put them on the floor by her feet.

"And a book." He held it out.

God, what a fool he must look. Offering piddly little flowers and a book she'd probably already read.

Grace eyed the book then gasped, making him jolt. She snatched the book from him and flicked it open. "A History of Cats." She looked up at him. "Wherever did you find this?"

HIS BASHFUL SMILE softened her heart. Even though she knew it was not physically possible, Grace swore she felt an actual softening, as though the muscle was turning to mush.

She flicked open the book and scanned a page, unable to keep the smile from her face. Apparently, Claude had softened toward him too and come out of wherever he was hiding to nibble on the meat. She closed the book, took the flowers, and inhaled the sweet fragrance.

"They're beautiful, thank you."

He shrugged. "I would have rather purchased a bouquet from a florist, but it was all I could do in a rush."

She peered at him. "You picked them yourself?"

He nodded, that bashful expression pulling at his lips again where usually a cocksure smile sat.

"Thank you," she repeated.

"I know I was an ass," he said quickly. "I didn't even try to understand what you are going through, what you've had to run away from."

"I was not exactly forthcoming about it."

"I realize you are scared but I was also scared. I did not want any harm to come to you."

She reached up and set the flowers on the table at the side of the bed then rested back against the bed frame. "I know you have a duty to protect me and I am sorry I did not think you could."

"Grace," he muttered, "it's more than damned duty. I would never forgive myself if anything happened to you."

She stole a sideways look at him. Did he mean it? Was she more than duty? Did he perhaps care for her even a little? She mentally shook herself. He was no fool or idle gentleman as she had said but he was just here because he was being paid to look after her and she would do well to remember that.

"I won't leave."

"Are you just saying that so I let down my guard and you can escape?"

She shook her head. "I know you are right. I would not survive on my own for long. That was one of the main reasons we needed your help. I have no one to go to and I was scared my aunt would come to harm should it be known I ran away voluntarily."

"Your uncle is that bad?" She caught him flex a fist out of the corner of her eye.

"He is selfish and cruel. He has never laid a hand on my aunt or I but there are many ways he could punish her. She lives on little but gives most generously, whilst he hoards everything and continues to accrue debt." He stiffened slightly beside her. She twisted to face him. "If I married Mr. Worthington, my uncle would take some of the inheritance as payment. I overheard him talking about it when Mr. Worthington first started calling on us."

"Bastard," he muttered.

"He isn't, technically," she pointed out. "He is of good stock. But I appreciate the sentiment."

"And this Worthington? He's harmed women before?"

"Of course it is only murmured about but he was known to discipline his wife. Then, one day, she was found at the bottom of the stairs—dead." Grace suppressed the shudder the image created. "It was said she tripped and fell but everyone believes he pushed her." She wrapped her hands around her waist. "I am not the easiest person to get along with. I have never been prepared to be a wife nor do I have any desire to cow to a man. How long would it be before I ended up at the bottom of the stairs?"

"I can see why you'd be afraid, but I promise you, Grace, so long as there is breath in my body, I will not let you come to harm."

She looked into his eyes and the mush that had become her heart sprung back to life, beating fiercely like a war drum. In the candlelight, he was more than beautiful. She could liken him to a work of art, yet she had never seen a portrait like this. The candlelight warmed his skin and brought out the sheen in his dark curls. A faint scar she had never noticed before curved down by his lip. She reached out for it before she had realized what she had done.

He flinched and she snapped her hand back, curling it protectively in the other. She wanted to touch his face again. Her fingers tingled with the need.

"How did you get that scar?" she blurted out. There was more she wished to ask. So many questions. But she feared scaring him away and right now, there was nowhere she wanted to be more than at his side, sitting on the floor by her bed.

His lips curled. "I lived a rather salubrious life in my youth. This was the result of quite the fight."

"You are strong, but I never pictured you as a fighter."

Nash's lips quirked. "You are quite the flatterer, Grace."

She frowned. "Did you wish me to say I could see you as a fighter?"

"I hope you never have to see me fight. It was not the prettiest of pictures. However, my ego will not let me ignore that you have noticed my strength."

"I do not see how you could enjoy such words. It is fact and you must know it."

He shook his head with a grin. "How little you know of men. We always enjoy compliments from pretty women."

Opening her mouth, she fought for an answer, then gave up and shut it again.

"You can say it you know, whatever it is you are feeling."

What she was feeling? Sweet Mary, she hardly knew. Her limbs were strangely weak, her head swirling with a strange sort of fog, thicker than the yellow smog that covered London in the morning. How could she possibly fathom what she was feeling?

"Grace?" he prodded.

"I...I suppose I like that you called me pretty."

"There, see. We both enjoy flattery."

Her gaze caught on his and she froze. Not a single muscle would respond to any commands, even more so when his gaze flicked down to her lips. The fog lifted, leaving a hot, brazen wash of air to sweep through her. She knew what this was. Logic dictated exactly what was to happen. His eyes had darkened, he was leaning in. Nash's gaze kept falling to her mouth.

She was going to be kissed.

Grace let her eyes flutter closed. She waited, breath held. Moments passed by and she heard the slight rustle of clothes and Claude nibbling on his food. She swallowed hard.

Something tapped her hand and she snapped open her eyes. Nash patted the back of her hand again and offered a slightly apologetic smile.

"It's late," he said, hastening to his feet. "I had better..." He stumbled over the edge of her blanket in his rush to get to the door.

She rose to her feet and watched him dash out of her room.

"Goodnight," he said, quickly ducking his head and not bothering to shut the door behind him.

She clapped a hand to the side of her face. What on earth had she done wrong to make him run away from her?

Chapter Twelve

Grace ticked off the little lines scored onto her notes with her fingers. Five, ten, fifteen...she frowned. That couldn't be right. Did she arrive here on the twelfth of February or the thirteenth? She looked over to Mary while she busied herself tugging off the sheets of Grace's bed.

"Did I come here on the twelfth or the thirteenth?"

Mary peered around the large white sheet. "I would ask Nash. I'm terrible at dates."

Grace made a face. Not that she did not wish to see Nash, but she did not want to ask him because if she did, he would ask her why she wanted to know, and she would have to explain why.

She was deathly bored.

By her calculations, she still had twenty days left here. Twenty long days. If only Nash had a calendar or something somewhere. Losing track of the days as one merged into another was driving her slightly addled.

"Is it Tuesday?" she asked.

"Yes," Mary said, slightly out of breath. She flung the sheet down onto the bed and grunted with effort as she tucked it in around the corners. Grace rose and helped with the other side.

"Twenty days then," she murmured to herself. Then she could leave and be independent and...and... "Oh."

Never see Nash again.

"What's the matter?" Mary asked.

Grace shook her head. "Nothing at all. Do you need some more help? I could help make Nash's bed." She wrinkled her nose. "If that is not too much of an intrusion."

"I doubt Nash will mind but I have already done it."

"Perhaps there is some food I can help you with? Or dusting perhaps? Maybe I could chop something." She made a chopping motion with her hands.

Mary laughed. "I'm afraid I have prepared everything for dinner already, but you can help me tomorrow. Do you have much experience cooking?"

"Not really," Grace admitted. Though, she should get some experience, even if she would be able to afford a cook once she gained her inheritance. She had always thought she had quite a varied knowledge but after her time here, she realized it was rather limited to intellectual pursuits rather than practical. It might be quite pleasant to know she could do a few things for herself. Maybe she would not feel so vulnerable then.

"Well, I can guide you but I'm afraid that shall have to wait. Once I am finished here, I must return home. My brothers are bound to fight over the chores if I am not there to stop them."

"Do you like working here? And on the farm?"

Mary cocked her head. "Why? Are you looking for a job?"

Grace knew it was ridiculous, a woman like her even considering physical labor. And she wasn't, not really. But in some ways, she envied Mary. She came and went as she pleased and always seemed content. "I was just curious."

"I enjoy cooking. Cleaning, not so much. But Nash pays me well and it gives me a little bit of independence. As for the farm, it is hard work, but it is *ours*, and will be our children's one day."

"I understand. Having independence must be nice."

Mary smiled. "You shall have it soon enough."

But what would she do with it?

"If you are bored, why do you not ask Nash if you can go for a walk or something?"

"I'm not certain he will let me," she said, knowing it was an excuse. What if someone spotted her? What if her uncle's men had somehow discovered her location and snatched her and took her back home?

"He is not an ogre." Mary made a shooing motion. "Go and ask him."

Grace trudged out of the room. She did not think for one minute Nash was an ogre. He always seemed quite chipper. The fact he had ever spent time fighting still baffled her. She had thought to make a note of the fact but at this point, her notes were so wild and jumbled, she could not make head nor tail of them.

Nash remained a great mystery to her.

She found him outside, tugging on some of the vines that were crawling across one of the front windows to a room he kept closed off. She went onto tiptoes to peer in but could only see sheets covering various bits of furnishings.

"What are you doing?" she asked.

He ceased pulling on the vine and swiped his hands down his trousers. "Thought I might make myself useful. These vines are beginning to swallow the place."

His slightly bashful expression had her insides doing that funny thing again, turning to liquid then to something warm and strange, flowing down into her limbs. She eyed his gloved hands where they curled firmly about the weed then followed the line of his arms, up to his rolled shirtsleeves.

Arms were just, well, arms, but on Nash they seemed to be a whole different thing. They were slightly sunkissed, probably from riding, she concluded, and covered in fine, dark hair. Probably soft to the touch.

"Did you need something?" he pressed.

She snapped her gaze back to his face. "Oh, I was just...um...looking for something to do."

"You can help here if you wish. Though you might want to change."

She glanced down at her plain muslin. "I realized the other day when I went to pack that I didn't bring anything with me. It is either this or that dress Mary gave me, and I think this is not as fine."

"You'll get dirty," he warned.

"It doesn't matter."

"Take this bit then." He handed over the length of vine. "And I shall pull from behind you."

She nodded, licking her dry lips and catching her reflection in the dirty window. She spotted him behind, towering above her, his body lined up behind her. The image made her stomach twist and dance and she smelled his cologne, a fresh, spicy scent which made her skin prick. He was close, so close. Just a little move backward and she would be in his arms.

What a far-too-delicious thought that was.

NASH SHOULD HAVE declined. Said no. Told her to scram. *Nein. No. Nyet.*

It would have been easy enough. But, no, he had to ask her to help and put himself in such a position that he was struggling hard to control his body.

He peered at the top of her head. There was nothing exciting about the top of a head, he told himself. In fact, Grace went out of her way to make the top of her head exceedingly dull. He never once saw her with an elaborate hairstyle or some curls gracefully touching her skin. Her dark, glossy hair remained tied tightly in a no-fuss sort of a knot and a parting down the center, revealing a pale line of scalp.

Exceedingly dull really.

However, being so close to her was anything but dull and no matter how much he considered how unexciting her hair was, his body would not listen.

Drawing in a long breath, he gripped the vine in his gloved hands. He'd had some thoughts that doing a little physical labor might dampen his needs but even after an hour of ripping and pulling at weeds, his desire would not be abated.

And there was no denying it now. Hell, he'd almost kissed her the other night. She'd been ready for it too, eyes closed, lips pursed. It would have been so damned easy to take what he wanted.

"Hold it firmly," he ordered, groaning inwardly at the image *that* created. "And give it a little tug at first."

Good Lord, what the devil was wrong with him?

He closed his mouth and they pulled on the vine together. The stubborn plant refused to give way, so he let go and used his knife to cut away some of the smaller offshoots that clung stubbornly to the window.

"This is harder than I thought," she commented.

He stared at her.

"What's wrong?"

Nash shook his head and took up his position behind her again. The woman had no idea what she was doing to him. First, he'd nearly broken his promise to the others that he would never, ever touch any of the women in his protection, and now he had taken up manual labor in some odd bid to impress her. The fact was, her words still grated—the idea that he did nothing aside from sit around and play the country gent.

Of course, her words still grated because they were somewhat true. He did whatever he could for these women and was not unproud of helping them but his role as protector had never meant doing much. He'd certainly never had to worry about awful uncles or violent fiancés potentially chasing them down.

He could not help but wonder if, perhaps, his father had been right too. He hadn't done much with his life and would have continued to remain aimless had they not fallen out.

Nash clenched his jaw and pulled hard on the vine. It gave way too quickly, and Grace stumbled backward with a squeak. The air flew from Nash's lungs when his back struck the ground and a sharp elbow landed in his gut.

She rolled, her face mere inches from his. "I am so sorry." She shoved a strand of hair from her face. "So, so sorry."

"It was my fault. I pulled too hard."

"I should have had firmer footing. Of course, you would pull hard. You have more strength than I do."

She said it so matter-of-factly that he couldn't even find it in himself to be flattered by her words. Not that he needed words at this point. He was far too focused on the fact that her slender body was atop him, aligned perfectly with one knee cradled between his legs and the other straddling his hip. From her wide eyes, he knew she had little idea the position she had put herself in.

She rose up, one hand to his chest. "Are you quite well? Did I hurt you?"

"I am fine," he said with a grunt, trying to focus on the patch of white sky behind her and most certainly not on the line of her waist or the arch of her neck or, hell, even her fingers and how they were splayed upon his torso.

"I never meant to hurt you."

"You did not hurt me," he insisted through clenched teeth.

Oh, but parts of him were hurting and if she remained there much longer, she would find out. But for some reason, his body refused to move. All he needed to do was gently ease her off him. Instead, he was lying here like an invalid, desperately trying to control his cock.

"You seem a little dazed." She touched his forehead then trailed her fingers down his temple, looking deep into his eyes. "Your pupils look a little dilated."

Yes, because you are so bloody close, he wanted to say. Because every breath he took hurt. Because he'd never had to fight so hard to maintain control.

"I am fine," he repeated.

Grace flicked her gaze over him. "Perhaps you should lie still for a minute. I could get a cold compress or—"

He grabbed the hand that lingered on his face. "No."

"But you could be hurt and not know it. You might have struck a rock or—"

"No."

"Lift your head a little and let me see if you have hurt yourself." She leaned forward, allowing him a glance between the thick fabric of her fichu and the plain neckline of her gown.

He groaned. Good God.

"See? you are hurt!"

He gripped both her arms and eased her up. "I am not hurt, and you must get off immediately."

"Let me at least—" She tried to reach for the back of his head.

"God damn it, woman, bloody get off!"

She froze, her eyes wide. "I'm sorry, I did not mean to hurt you."

"I am not bloody well hurt." He ground his teeth together, drawing in hot breaths through his nostrils. "But you must remove yourself immediately, Grace."

"But—"

"Immediately," he insisted.

"Oh." Her throat worked and her eyes widened further. She glanced down between them. "*Oh!*"

Grace scrabbled off, a flurry of skirts, muttered apologies, and pink cheeks.

Nash threw an arm over his face, unable to watch her scarper off. He glanced down at where his arousal tented his trousers. At least he didn't have to worry about keeping his distance from her, he supposed. He'd terrified her enough that she would likely hide away in her room for the rest of her stay here.

Chapter Thirteen

Grace shoved aside the bundle of paper. It was no good. No matter how much she wrote or pondered on the matter, she could not figure out Nash.

Or more to the point, she could not figure out his, erm, arousal situation.

Every time she closed her eyes at night, she recalled his body pressing hard against hers. A mere glance at him had a rush of sensation, twisting, burning, coiling through her, until it became hard to breathe and every part of her heated. Most especially where their bodies had connected.

It was biology, remember?

Oh, well, her body remembered, and it did not matter how many times she told herself that she was a healthy female and he a healthy male and it was natural for nature to persuade them they should procreate.

There was no forgetting the moment.

She suspected Nash had not forgotten either which was strange. A man like Nash was bound to be experienced and had likely made love to many a woman. Why a little moment of arousal should embarrass him she could not be certain. He didn't seem to be the sort to be embarrassed. But, then, as she had already concluded, she could not fathom him.

Or herself, apparently, because at this very moment, a jolt of something sharp dug into her chest, like the prick of a needle, at the thought of him making love to other women.

She glanced his way and tried to force aside the picture of him doing exactly what they were doing at present with another woman. Why should it matter that he had looked after others? That he had done anything so simple as sat in a drawing room, on two opposite sides of the room, whilst he read his newspaper by candlelight and she pretended to be occupied with her notes at the small table by the window.

It did not matter. Logically and for any other reason. It absolutely did not matter.

In which case, she did not need to ask about them.

Most certainly not.

"Nash?"

Curses, what was wrong with her?

He folded down the corner of the paper to peer at her. "Grace?"

Well, she was committed now. So why not ask the questions? Maybe it would help her understand why she was feeling this way. She doubted it but one could only hope.

She twisted around on the chair to face him. "Have you, um, looked after many women...in this way? That is, with the kidnapping, not in any other way, you understand, but just like this...like how we are doing..." She twined her hands together in her lap and cast her gaze down. This was not at all how one conducted an investigation, of that she was certain.

"Yes, there have been several."

"Oh."

She knew that, so why on earth was she disappointed?

"Were they...beautiful?"

Oh Lord, that was not the intended question. Looks had nothing to do with anything. She did not hold them much in high regard. At least, perhaps, she had not until meeting Nash. She had to admit to finding his good looks extremely attractive but, also, she suspected, it did not help that she rather liked the man beneath. He seemed to just move through life without considering anything and she admired his boldness. She couldn't recall a single time when she had not contemplated even the simplest of decisions.

A dark brow rose. "Some, yes."

"Why did they come to you?"

He folded the paper and set it aside on the sofa. "I don't think I should be discussing their affairs with you, Grace."

"No, of course."

Inwardly, she cringed. Naturally, he could not, and as playful as he could be, she knew he would not compromise his honor. The fact that he had pushed her away when he had become aroused made that obvious. A man like Nash could have any woman he wanted. It would have been easy for him to seduce her.

So easy.

She resisted the desire to clap hands to her cheeks. Good Lord, this was more than a simple biological desire. She felt it, deep, deep down, this need to touch and taste and feel his body against hers. To explore his unique maleness and study him so, so much closer.

"They all needed help, is all I can say. Some needed to escape to make a new life, some were in slightly similar situations to you."

She forced a smile and pushed away the ghosts of beautiful women breezing about the drawing room in their elegant way. Grace was never one for comparisons, but it was no good, that silly emotion that was jealousy was working its way deep. If this were a mere desire to breed, surely she would not be feeling such things?

"I am sure they are most grateful for your aid," she said tightly.

"I was glad to help them."

"And to be paid."

Now why did she feel the need to say that? Would it put distance between them somehow, if she reminded herself that once she gained her inheritance, she would owe these kidnappers a healthy sum.

He chuckled. "That does not hurt either." He pointed to the roof. "In case you had not noticed, this house does rather need the funds."

She glanced up toward the damp patch that stained one corner. "How exactly did this house get in such a state?"

"It's rather simple really. I lack money and this house costs a lot of it."

"But you must come from wealth, surely? You are heir to a title after all."

"Grace, you are a clever woman. You know that not all nobility have the wealth to match their titles."

"Yes, I suppose I do." But the answers still explained little about him. "But how did you come to have no wealth? And where is your family? Your father cannot be dead if you have not inherited."

His posture changed again, his jaw hardening. "My father is alive and the rest of it is a long story." He smiled quickly. "Let us talk on nicer matters. Like, your own fortune, for example. What a boon that shall be once you have inherited."

THE DISAPPOINTMENT IN her expression didn't pass Nash's notice. However, the last thing he wanted to do was indulge her curiosity about him. The less she knew, the better. And, damn it, for the first time ever, he was feeling mightily ashamed of his past indiscretions. How could he explain his lack of fortune and this crumbling house was all down to him? Down to his greed? The very thing she loathed her uncle for.

He'd always thought his father to blame for his current situation but now that he considered explaining it to someone—someone as good and wholesome and clever as Grace—it seemed ridiculous.

No one put the cards in his hand. No one forced him to bet money he didn't have.

He blew out a breath. Still, it did not mean his father had to cut him off in such a way and break his promises to fix Guildham House. He loved this house and had dreamed for years of returning it to its former glory. Now that chance was gone. He couldn't forgive that.

"What shall you do once you are free of your uncle?" he asked. It was much better that he think of her future too. A future without him. Then perhaps he could get his damned desires under control. Not much longer and she'd be deposited home, of age, and fully independent.

And nowhere near him.

"You know I hope to set up a home with my aunt."

"But what else?"

She opened her mouth, closed it, and frowned.

"You must have some other ambitions. Or someone you are interested in perhaps," he forced himself to ask, knowing if she answered in the positive it would be more painful than he was willing to admit.

"Interested?"

"Someone other than that bastard Worthington?"

"Oh." She shook her head vigorously. "I have had little to do with society and I doubt I would garner anyone's attention even if I had." She lifted a shoulder. "Besides, I have no interest in gaining a husband."

"Your inheritance may change that."

"I doubt that."

Nash curled a hand around the arm of the sofa. It was all he could do to keep from standing up, striding over, and giving her a good, long shake. He couldn't blame the men in Town for missing this beauty due to her being hidden away but when it became known she was an heiress with reasonable wealth to her name, they would certainly pay attention. And, if they were clever, they would see that they were not only getting a wealthy wife, but a smart and beautiful one too.

He smirked to himself. Smart, in many ways perhaps, but entirely ignorant as to how appealing she was. Even after the other day, she kept blinking at him, that little furrow appearing between her brow, as though she could not fathom why having her on top of him had summoned an erection that had taken two cold baths to rid himself of.

"So you and your aunt shall live tucked away in the country somewhere? And do what with yourselves?"

She blinked a few times. God's teeth, why did he find the way she blinked so unnerving? He wanted to delve in there and pull whatever thoughts were rioting around her mind out. No doubt there were many. One could practically see Grace's mind ticking over, like the cogs of a clock, if one looked hard enough. He suspected the woman never once did anything spontaneous or without thinking hard about it first.

"I suppose I might get another cat..."

"That's it? Your grand plan is to get another cat?"

She folded her arms. "I had not really thought much farther than avoiding marrying a murderer and getting away from my uncle if I am honest."

"Well, at least be ambitious. Why not get five cats?"

"I might very well do that."

"And a goat."

"That too."

"You can have the peacock if you wish."

Her chin lifted. "I could provide him an excellent home I am sure."

Yes, no doubt, she could provide them all a loving home where she would write about them and study them and figure out their inner nature and pander to them perfectly.

Good Lord, he was jealous of a peacock and goat and a fictional group of cats.

"Sounds like an excellent plan," he muttered.

She huffed and unfolded her arms. "I cannot help that I am boring, Nash. I am sorry I do not have a crumbling mansion and a mysterious past." She lifted her hands. "This is me. I have little ambition and I like animals. That is it. I am boring."

Nash rose to his feet before he had quite fathomed what he was doing. He strode over and took her elbows in his hands, drawing her up to meet him. Her lips parted and her eyes widened.

"What are you—?"

"Do not ever say that again," he said firmly.

"But—"

"You are far, far, far from boring."

He curled a hand around her neck and kissed her. Hard. It took all of two seconds. Two mere seconds and they were pressed together, her lips beneath his. Two seconds to break all of his silent promises to himself, to Grace, and all those very real promises he had made to Guy.

She tasted so damned good, he couldn't bring himself to regret it.

After a little squeak of surprise, she settled against him, and he wrapped an arm around her waist to bring her closer. Her fingers dug into his upper arms while he explored her lips with his—only briefly, long enough to gain entrance.

She made another sound, one that tugged deep inside him and made him harder than a stone statue. Her body softened further, and he gripped her to him tight, pushing the kiss hard and deep, sweeping his tongue into her mouth with a groan.

It was no good. He was lost to her.

EVEN IF GRACE had her notes to hand, she was not certain she would be able to put the kiss into words.

Warm perhaps. Soft. But not soft.

Hard, firm, demanding.

But his lips were soft.

It was such a strange concoction of opposites.

She finally settled on delicious.

Yes, that sounded right. Delicious covered it in so many ways without it being too specific. His arms wrapped about her was a delicious sensation. He *tasted* delicious. And the feeling inside her could be classed as that too. Utterly, completely delicious.

She had never been kissed before unless she counted when Robert Fletcher pressed a slimy kiss to her cheek when her father was still alive but she had a strong suspicion there were not many men who could kiss and make it so...so...*delicious*.

Nash eased his grip on her neck then loosened his hold on her waist. When he moved back and broke the kiss, she could not hold back the satisfied sigh that escaped her.

"Well, that was nice," she said softly.

"Nice?" he echoed, his voice slightly choked.

"Indeed." She nodded. "You are an excellent kisser."

He stared at her as though she had sprouted horns or turned into Claude.

"I cannot have been the first woman to say that..."

"No." He rubbed a hand across his face. "That is..." He took a few steps away from her. "Grace, I..."

His shirtsleeves were crumpled from where she'd gripped him so tightly. It made her want to grab them again and haul him back to her.

How many times would she relive that kiss in the future? And if she did it again, would it be different this time? What was a gentler kiss like? What was it like to kiss lying down? She had seen it illustrated in books that she most certainly should not have read but if one was to fully understand humans or animals, one had to understand the basic mechanics of procreation as far as she was concerned.

"Stop it," he said abruptly.

"Stop what?"

"Thinking."

"Thinking? What do you mean?"

"I can see it." He made a twirling motion with a finger. "I can see your brain working behind those big eyes. It's enough to drive a man mad."

She scowled. "Thinking can drive a man mad?"

"Yes. No." He blew out a breath. "It's the content of your thoughts," he explained.

"How can you possibly know the contents of my thoughts?"

"Your eyes go wider, and you blink a lot. It usually means you are having complex thoughts that should never, ever be said aloud."

"Goodness." Was she so obvious? That was a little disconcerting. Surely he could not tell that she was wondering how it would feel if she touched him more? If she just slipped a hand inside his shirt and felt the warmth of his—

"Stop it, damn it."

"Goodness," she murmured again.

"That's putting it mildly."

"Well, I am very sorry if I have embarrassed you."

He chuckled. "Grace, I am certainly not embarrassed, but you must cease your thoughts." He shook his head in dismay and she realized her mind had slipped, following her gaze down the length of him. She snapped her gaze to his and laced her fingers demurely together.

"I am here to look after you, nothing else. I most certainly should not have kissed you."

"But as I said it was—"

"Nice, I know."

He uttered the word as though she had said something horrible like...like *turd*.

"Regardless, if it was nice, I should not have done it."

"There is no harm," she insisted. "I am not scandalized or upset. I won't tell anyone."

"But I'll know." He prodded his chest with a finger. "I am many things, Grace, but I do not break promises, and I vowed I would not touch you."

"Vowed to whom?"

"The others, The Kidnap Club."

She swallowed as a knot jarred itself in the top of her throat. "Do you...do you make a habit of, um, touching the other women?"

"Of course not."

If she had a chair nearby, she might have collapsed into relief. Preposterous really. Nash had no doubt kissed and made love to many women in his past, but she loathed the thought of him kissing the other women who had stood in her shoes.

"So why would you need to make such a vow?"

His lips slanted. "I have a reputation as somewhat of a rake, Grace. I am surprised you have not figured that out by now."

"I can see that you might be considered as such, but you have done nothing that would make me think you might take advantage of a woman. In fact, you have been nothing but kind and gentlemanly."

He grimaced. "If you think your thoughts are salacious, you would be shocked by mine."

"Oh."

"And I would never take advantage of a woman. Ever. But in this situation, it would be too easy for you to fall for me."

"Fall for you?"

"I am your protector, your shoulder to cry on. The one rescuing you from your awful predicament."

She peered at him. "I *am* paying you to rescue me, so I am not wholly certain it counts as rescuing."

"My point is, I cannot kiss you again. I *will* not kiss you again."

"It seems a shame really. I think we were quite good at it."

Chapter Fourteen

Nice. Even now the word stung.

Nice.

The understatement of the decade.

No, the century.

Nice.

Nash curled his lip and closed the door to the stables. The word echoed with his footsteps back to the house. *Nice, nice, nice, nice.* It hadn't left him since last night. Every creak he heard, every time he tossed in his bed and the bed frame rattled, it hissed it at him, like a jeer.

Nice.

That kiss had been more than nice. It had been compelling, enticing, delectable, titillating...anything but nice.

It had also been wrong. As he had reminded Grace, he was many things, but he never went back on his word, and he loathed anyone who did so. He knew all too well how a promise broken could ruin everything, including family relationships.

So was it not better that she thought it simply nice?

Though, from the way he'd seen her mind working, he suspected she had been working on other ways to explore how nice the kiss was. He couldn't deny he was doing the same but at least he managed to keep the thoughts to himself. Knowing she was picturing them together was pure and utter torture.

He strode into the house, grunting a greeting at Mary as she bustled by with an armful of linen.

"Nash, the food arrived today, and I've put a fresh newspaper in the drawing room for you."

He paused and muttered a thank you. If Mary thought him rude, she would not be wrong, but she said nothing. He took the stairs two at a time. The last thing he had time for was discussing the food delivery or the latest newspaper. Especially not when he was in danger of embarrassing himself most sincerely thanks to Grace.

"Grace!" he spluttered, nearly running into her at the top of the stairs.

"Sorry." She took a few steps back and peered over her shoulder toward the left wing of the house. Her cheeks were pink, even in the dark light of the hallway.

"What are you doing?"

Apart from driving him to the edge of insanity that was.

"Oh, well..." She rocked on her heels. "I was a little bored, you see, and you were out riding so..."

"So...?"

She pursed her lips. He groaned inwardly and focused on the patch of wall behind her where the tapestry had frayed at the edges. Nothing exciting at all. Completely and utterly dull. No lips, no mouths, nothing tempting.

Because he absolutely would not, most definitely kiss her again. If he did, he could say goodbye to this income and most likely his friends too. He rubbed a hand over his jaw. If this continued, he'd have to admit to Russell he was struggling. Maybe he could come and watch over her instead.

No, he didn't want Russell alone with her. The man might not be charming, but he was clever and handsome. Then Grace might want to kiss him instead and there was no way in hell Nash was letting that happen.

Kisses. Lips. Mouth. Grace's mouth. His gaze landed on it again and he caught the last of what she was saying.

"...a look."

"Pardon?"

"I was hoping I might have a look." She motioned down the hallway. "At the east wing?" she explained when he stared at her blankly. "I tried the door, but it is locked."

"Ah." He patted the pocket of his waistcoat. "I have the key, somewhere."

"I thought perhaps you might not want me to look. In case there was something you did not want me seeing."

He tugged out the small set of keys. Mary kept the larger set on her person, but he had a few in case he needed to go into any of the other rooms.

"Did you think perhaps I have a wife hidden in one of the rooms? Or a hideously disfigured relative?"

She shook her head. "I know you keep them locked because they are derelict, but you are less than forthcoming with information about yourself. One cannot help think you might have a little something to hide."

Only a past that he was becoming increasingly uncomfortable with.

"There is little to tell," he said blithely. "An education at Cambridge, some time spent in London, and then I joined The Kidnap Club."

Her eyes narrowed. "I think there must be more to you than that."

"Nothing of note, I can assure you."

Unless one counted lots of debts, too much time at the gaming tables, and a father who cut him off.

He opened the door to the east wing, leaving it ajar so the light could penetrate the long, dark hallway. It smelled of must and damp. He moved in front of her, easing her back with a hand to her arm. "I haven't been in here in a few months so be careful. The floor is rotten in a few places."

"What a shame this house is suffering. It would be so sad to see it fall apart."

He nodded. It would. He'd spent several happy summers here as a boy until his father had purchased a house closer to the coast. Then the building had been forgotten about.

Just as he had.

"I intend to see it all repaired but as you can imagine, it would cost a large sum, and I am rather in want of funds at present." He took her hand to lead her down the corridor. "I always loved this house." He smiled. "One day, though, I shall see it restored to its former glory."

"THAT SOUNDS LOVELY. But why does no one else care for this house?"

His jaw tightened and Grace almost regretted the question. She saw the love and admiration in his face for the house whenever he spoke of it. She had to wonder why his father, wherever he was, did not get involved in repairing a house that must be worth a fortune.

"For some reason, I am the only one in my family with any attachment to it. I suppose it is because I was here a lot when my parents were travelling."

She nodded and peered down the darkened corridor. A whistle of wind echoed down in and she stilled. "Perhaps this is not such a good idea. There might be rats."

"I thought you liked animals."

"Rats are rodents."

"You said the floors are rotten, what if we fall through a hole?"

"I said this floor is. The lower floor is still in excellent condition."

"When did you last step foot in there again?"

"A few months ago," he replied casually.

"So there could be holes there now."

"It would not deteriorate that quickly." He shook his head with a grin. "Come now, do you not trust me to keep you safe?"

She pursed her lips and looked into the darkened shadows of his face where she could just make out his amused gaze. "There is nothing wrong with being cautious, you know."

"Not at all. So long as it does not prevent one from enjoying life to the fullest."

"Are you ever cautious, Nash?"

He took a moment before answering, "Probably not."

"You really should try it sometimes."

"Just as you should try to be bolder at times." He tugged on her hand. "Come on, this shall be worth it, I promise."

"Very well." She allowed him to guide her down the darkened staircase. "Though, I should like to point out that it is all very easy for you to talk about taking chances."

He aided her down the last step into the gloom. A little sliver of light escaped from around a door ahead of them, guiding them forward. "How so?"

"Well, you are a man, and you are strong, and from a good family. I assume. You are allowed to be bold."

He stopped by the door. "I suppose you are right." Turning the knob, he pushed it open and she blinked in the sudden light.

Any thoughts of boldness or caution left her when she peered into the room. A grand ballroom spread out before her. Though shutters concealed every tall window, a huge glass dome that mimicked the one in the entrance hall let in swathes of beautiful colored light. She slipped her hand out of Nash's and stepped forward, her shoes tapping on the marbled floor until she reached the center of the room, right beneath the dome. She craned her neck to make out the stained-glass patterns above.

"This is beautiful."

He joined her in the middle of the room. "Yes, it is."

She glanced down to find him staring at her. Her throat tightened and she fought to draw in her next breath.

Looking quickly away, he gestured around the room. "It didn't see many balls when I was younger, but my grandfather spent most of his time in the country and preferred to host them here."

"It seems such a shame this space is not used."

"I hope to put it to use one day."

Grace peered down at where her shoes peeked out from her hem. She did not much want to think about Nash dancing around the ballroom with some elegant woman on his arm. A woman who would most likely be his wife. After all, nobility had to marry at some point.

She moved away from him in a bid to escape the silly jealousy pouring through her. She had no claim over this man and had anyone asked her a few weeks ago if she had ever experienced the emotion, she would have decried it as a waste of time.

It still was. As tired and as old as this building was, it was a reminder of the differences between them. He was bold, she was cautious. She came from a simple life, he did not. He would go on to be a lord one day while she would find herself tucked away with her aunt somewhere, likely living the life of a spinster.

She did a circle of the room and stopped by a family portrait. Their clothing appeared relatively modern, so she had to assume the painting was not old. "Who is this?"

Nash took her hand to lead her away. "No one in particular."

She rooted her feet and studied the painting. Two parents, three children—one older girl, a little boy who could not be more than two years of age, and a baby in the mother's arms. She leaned in to look closer. "Is this little boy you?"

"Yes, handsome little fellow, was I not? Now, let us take a look—"

"And these are your parents, and your siblings?"

"Yes, yes," he said, impatience edging his voice.

"I did not know you had siblings."

"It never really came up." He tried to pull her away again. "Why do we not—"

"Why would you not mention such a thing?"

He blew out a breath. "Because it does not matter, Grace. I do not see them and that is all there is to it."

"You don't see your family? Any of them?"

"No," he snapped. "Not my father, not my mother, not my sisters."

"Oh." She tilted her head. "But why?"

He dropped her hand. "None of them like me very much, that is why. Now, shall we continue?"

So much of her wished to ask more but his tense posture and hard jaw prevented her. For some reason, Nash did not wish to share anything about his family with her. What secret was he hiding?

Chapter Fifteen

"Bloody hell," Nash muttered under his breath. He shoved back his blankets and rose from bed, putting a hand to the post of the bed and battling with the curtains around it to escape.

When he finally freed himself, he blinked in the darkness, trying to fathom the source of the sound. It had definitely been a crash of some kind, something falling or breaking perhaps. But he couldn't see any sign of anything once his eyes had adjusted.

He stilled.

Bloody hell.

Grace.

Someone had found them. Someone was trying to get to her.

He'd damn well kill them.

He raced out of the bedroom and barged through her door, fists raised. The window was ajar, curtains blowing in the aggressive wind. He heard the splatter of rain upon the glass. But there was no one.

No one except Grace huddled on her bed, her knees pulled up against her chest, her eyes wide. He released a breath and lowered his fists. "What happened?"

"The...the wind. It must have blown open the window."

He moved over to the window to see the pane had cracked with the force of the wind and the lock had broken away from the wood frame. Once he had retrieved a taper and lit a candle, he spied broken glass near the side of her bed.

"Do not move," he ordered.

She shook her head vigorously.

Thankfully the window had not entirely shattered and only a few large shards of glass sat beneath the window. He hated to think what might have happened had it shattered completely. Grace could have been severely hurt. Damn it, he should have checked the room better, ensured it was in good repair.

At least it was not what he had thought, and her wretched fiancé had not come to steal her away from him.

That was, from this house.

Not from him. He didn't own her.

His insides itched uncomfortably with the knowledge that a strong part of him would very much like to own her. To have the freedom to kiss her and touch her and listen to all her insistent questions and encourage her to take a chance every now and then.

He scooped up the few shards and tucked them into a handkerchief then set it on the small table by the fireplace. Finally, he turned to Grace. Still curled up in a tiny ball, her eyes wide, her skin pale. She shivered and gripped her legs tighter.

"You cannot stay here," he said. "You'll freeze. Let us get you into one of the other bedrooms and I'll have a fire lit."

"I-I do not think I can move."

"I've cleared away the glass, you shall be quite safe from harm."

She shook her head.

Frowning, Nash eased down onto the bed beside her, his weight on the mattress making it sink so that she ended up leaning into him. He snatched a blanket from the bottom of the bed and pulled it up over her. "Grace?"

Her wide gaze met his. "I thought..." She inhaled a shuddery breath. "I thought it was my uncle. Or Mr. Worthington come to get me."

"I thought that for a moment too."

Her chin quivered. "I was so scared and all I could do was sit here, frozen."

He looped an arm around her shoulder to draw her close. "You're safe now," he soothed. "I will never, ever let anything happen to you."

It was a lie, of course. Once she turned one and twenty, this would be over, and he'd likely never see her again. What happened to her in future would not be up to him.

She nodded, pressing her face into his chest and curling her fingers around the collar of his shirt as though it was a lifeline. He concentrated carefully on taking steady breaths and ignoring the brush of her fingers against his bare skin. Now was most certainly not the time to think about how he was only wearing a shirt with nothing beneath it and she was in a mere slip of shift and from what he had seen of her before, she wouldn't have anything on underneath it either.

Not the time at all.

His breaths grew hotter, the hairs on the back of his neck pricked. Good God, what a cad he was. Here she was, terrified, and he could only think about how easy it would be to slip a hand up her thighs and find out exactly what was beneath the white fabric.

"I bet you are never scared of anything," she murmured against his chest.

"Not at all." He rubbed her shoulder with his free hand. "I was extremely scared something had happened to you only moments ago."

She lifted her head and peered up at him. The wind tugged at the loose strands of hair around her face and her eyes glistened. "In truth?"

"In truth," he said solemnly.

"I know it is your job to look out for me, but I cannot help but like it," she confessed.

"I like it too," he admitted softly.

Her mouth parted and her tongue darted out briefly to sweep over her bottom lip. Never before had he envied a tongue, but he did right now. He wanted to be the one tasting her, exploring her mouth. He wanted it more than his next, uncomfortable, heated breath.

Grace didn't move, even though she had to know what was coming. Here she was scolding herself for being scared yet she had little idea how her courage was becoming the undoing of him.

"Why is it so hard to resist you?" he muttered gruffly, before lowering his mouth to hers.

THIS WAS A different sort of a kiss. It was tender, soft, seeking. The wind from the broken window breezed over her skin, bringing welcome relief from the heat boiling inside her. Nash tasted her as though she were some rare delicacy. It was enough to make her head spin and any thoughts of her uncle or anyone trying to take her away fled. All that remained was Nash.

Nash's arms around her. Nash's firm chest under her fingers. Nash's tongue seeking her own.

She splayed her fingers over the warm skin of his collarbone then down, smoothing over the crisp hair there. Sweet sensations swirled through her and down, pooling low, low, low. Behind her closed lids, she was lost to a world of desire, a world where she was so much more than a cold, small, shivering woman scared by a bit of wind.

In Nash's arms, she was desired, powerful. When she moved her fingers, he shivered, and if she pressed the kiss deeper, he groaned. To think she had power over this handsome, bold man was astonishing and she was hungry for more.

She shifted closer, pressing her breasts against his chest. The tips ached all the more at the contact, yet it brought some relief at the same time. He groaned again, bringing his hand up to her face to keep her close while he explored her mouth. His hand slipped down and around, under her arm to feel between them. A warm palm settled over her breast and she sighed, relaxing into the hold.

He smoothed and cupped and palmed and she tilted her head back. He trailed his lips down her neck, causing tremors to trip down her spine. Eyes still closed, she waited, breath held, while he moved his mouth farther, skipping over her collarbone then nuzzling to her breasts. The warm heat of his mouth over the fabric covering her nipples made her gasp. He grazed over it with his teeth then sucked.

Sweet Mary, no amount of reading books could have prepared her for this! She opened her eyes to watch him taste her through the fabric, one breast, then the next. She'd never understood what books meant by painting images as erotic, but she knew now.

And she'd never forget this.

She coiled her fingers through the silky soft strands of his dark hair and closed her eyes again. Who knew what would happen next but for once in her life, she did not care. She was willing to go forth with Nash, without reason, without thought.

The door squeaked and the bed dipped slightly. Heavy paws kneaded their way onto her lap, and Nash stilled. Reluctantly, Grace opened her eyes to find Claude settling on her lap between them. The cat lifted his hind leg oh so elegantly and began cleaning his nether regions.

"I suppose I should be thanking you," Nash muttered to the cat. He straightened, easing away from her.

"Thanking him?"

"Much longer and I might well have completely broken my vow not to touch you." He shoved a hand through his hair.

"I do believe you did touch me."

He grimaced. "I did. But no more, Grace." He shook a finger. "I really do not know why it is so hard to resist you."

She should have been insulted perhaps. After all, why would he be attracted to a skinny, boyish woman like her? However, if he had never touched any of the other women, that had to mean something, surely?

"We are designed to want to procreate." She patted the back of his arm. "It is only natural."

"I am not certain anything I feel for you is natural."

She scowled. "What on earth does that mean?"

"It means..." He shook his head. "Never mind." He eased off the bed and offered her a hand. "Let us get you settled in the other room. At least it is more than two doors away from me. Maybe the distance will help."

"Is it so wrong to want to kiss me?"

He eyed her. "Grace, I want to do more than kiss you, and, yes, it is very wrong. You are innocent, naïve."

She lifted her chin. "Not *that* naïve. I know how sex works."

He gave a dry chuckle. "Of course you do, but that does not mean you should partake in it. Especially not with someone like me."

"Someone like you?" she echoed.

"Someone who has vowed to behave where you are concerned. Someone who...well, it does not matter. Just trust me when I tell you your first time should certainly not be with me."

She took his hand and let him escort her to the other bedroom, Claude hooked in one arm. She had a thousand arguments running through her head but none of them were any better than *but I want to have my first time with you.*

Not very logical.

She certainly wouldn't win any arguments with that, especially seeing as he might very well be correct. He had some secrets and she was certain he'd been a rake in his past—all the indicators were there. Why else would his friends make him vow not to touch her? Really, he was doing the sensible thing.

For once in her life, she really, really did not want to do the sensible thing.

Nash lit the fire and checked the window was secure then turned to her where she stood, arms clasped around her waist, too aware that her nipples were still hard and the image of him *just there* would not leave her mind.

"Get into bed, Grace."

"I really do not want to."

"Do it," he ordered with a sigh.

She bit back her own sigh and padded across the room, settling under cold sheets. He gave one last reluctant look as he left the room. "Be a good girl and lock the door."

She opened her mouth to argue.

"I mean it."

Chapter Sixteen

"I unlocked my door."

Nash turned to find Grace in his bedroom doorway. He cursed silently. Two days and he had managed to resist kissing her again. But it had been damned hard.

"What are you doing here?"

"I've been thinking," she said as she shut the door behind her and turned to face him one more time.

"Always a dangerous thing," he murmured.

"Well, because I have been kidnapped people will make certain assumptions about me."

He frowned. "What do you mean?"

"The chances are, a young woman snatched by men would be, well, taken advantage of."

He let his scowl deepen.

"They will be ruined, Nash," she explained as though he was slow indeed.

Which he was feeling right now. Everything felt slow—his breaths, his movements. His ability to kick her out of his bedroom and away from danger.

"So?"

"So, it is clear to me, after some thought, that we are both feeling some sort of a reaction between us. For some reason, biology wants us to procreate."

He nearly choked on his breath. "Biology?"

"It means the science of life."

"Yes, I've heard of it before," he muttered. "But procreation?"

"Nash, I have little desire for a child."

"Then what..."

"Well, seeing as I will be ruined anyway it seems logical that I fornicate with you."

He stared at her for a few moments, taking in the utterly sensible expression to the innocently laced hands in front of her. Was he dreaming?

"Nash?" she prompted.

"What did you say again?"

"I wish to—how do you say it—bed you."

He swept a hand through his hair. "Good Lord."

"I am fairly certain you would not be averse to it."

He laughed dryly. That was an understatement. "Grace, you are an innocent and I—"

"I expect nothing from you," she said quickly, "apart from your expertise in the, um, fornication department."

"Dear God, please cease saying fornication."

"Sex then?"

Either way, it wasn't good. She offered herself up on a platter and he had little control in him to deny her.

Her throat worked and she reached behind her then turned slightly, peering at him over her shoulder. "Will you help me with the laces?"

He moved with leaden feet, unable to resist but knowing he intended to break the only firm promise he'd ever made.

"Stop," she said softly.

He halted, clenched his jaw. He stared at the laces in his hands. She twirled around to face him, and he let the laces fall from his grasp. Her fingers grazed across his jaw, drawing his gaze to hers. The milky expanse of one shoulder was just visible and his gaze darted down, drawn to the enchanting sight of bare skin.

Nash's hand shot out before he had even realized what he was doing and he let it linger above her shoulder, the desire to touch her making his skin itch. The heat of her skin seemed to penetrate the gap and his hand shook with restraint.

He had hated his father for breaking his vow to him. Was he really going to do the same?

"Have you...that is, do you not wish to touch me?"

He snapped his gaze to hers and noticed a hint of vulnerability dancing in her expression. "God," he rasped. "I want to touch you more than anything."

He closed the gap in a sudden rush of movement, and she gasped while he groaned at the feel of soft flesh under his hand. Who knew a damned shoulder could elicit such a reaction?

When she shifted her shoulder slightly, her gown slipped farther down one side, and became caught just above her breast. He spied the rosy edge of a nipple, just peeking over the edge of her stays.

Very well, apparently it was not just shoulders that were the undoing of him. Edges of nipples made his entire body heat too. He dipped a thumb underneath her gown and undergarments and rubbed unsteadily over her hardened nipple.

Grace sighed and closed her eyes as he caressed her breast. He found it hard to move away from this one breast, even knowing there was far, far more to explore. Maybe if he just stayed here, all would be well, and he wouldn't ruin her and wouldn't condemn himself.

With a slight shrug of her shoulder, her chemise slipped completely off her breast and he stared.

"I know men have a liking for large breasts but—"

Good Lord, this woman needed to turn her mind off for two seconds. A slight growl left him.

"But I have come to conclude you still want me." Her voice trembled slightly.

"I still want you. But you should not offer me this."

"It's entirely rational too, I assure you."

It did not make a difference how matter-of-factly she put it, he knew he shouldn't. But he'd be damned if he was going to deny her. Nash cursed and buried his fingers in her hair, pulling her to him for a kiss. He skimmed his lips over hers, nibbling and sucking, and he felt her tremble. The hard points of her nipples brushed his shirt and she moaned. He absorbed the moan, probing his tongue into her mouth and she met it eagerly.

Her hands skimmed down to his belt and she undid it slowly. It dropped to the floor with a thud and he drew back to allow her access to his shirt. Carefully, she loosened the laces at the neck, her gaze locked on his. As she leant forwards, he brushed a kiss across her forehead and swept his thumb over her cheek. Together, they yanked his shirt over his head, and she smiled at him.

Her fingers extended slowly out, playing across the coarse hair of his chest, tracing down the ridges of his stomach. Nash's muscles contracted under her touch and he sucked in a harsh breath. She studied him and he allowed it, offering himself up for her research of him. Her other hand joined in now, skating over his collarbone until she flattened both palms over his chest.

His throat worked as she traced her finger down it before placing a kiss at the base of his neck, where he felt his heart thud.

Nash needed to pull her gown fully off her. But he had yet to do so. Maybe, in the back of his mind, he thought he could still resist her.

Unlikely.

She must have sensed his uncertainty because she gently drew his hand toward the neckline of her gown, urging him to pull it the rest of the way down. His resistance crumbled and he tugged it down, along with her stays, revealing her other breast. Sweat pricked on his brow.

He shoved the fabric from her—the combination of stays, a chemise, and thick, unwieldy gown down. The last of his restraint dissipated then. How could he resist such an offering?

She shucked the rest of her clothing down and tugged off the stays with relish. He drew her to him, sucking in a sharp breath at the feel of her skin against his. She wriggled so her nipples rubbed across his chest.

Grace whimpered and he hissed as she shifted her hips, pushing against his agonizing arousal. He might well explode at any moment.

Dying to feel her against him in her entirety, he yanked off the rest of his clothes. He heard her breath catch and he stilled. Had he scared her?

Tentatively, she reached out and carefully explored the length of him. There was no embarrassment in her movements, just a chaste fascination. Nash restrained himself from thrusting into her hand, but she could never know how much willpower it took. He dare not frighten her away for it would likely be the death of him.

Her hand curled around him. "Did I do this to you?"

"Yes," he grated out.

Ever so slowly she released him, drawing her gaze back to his. "Touch me, Nash. I want to be yours."

"Yes," he growled and took her in his arms.

She buried her face into his neck, curled her fingers into his chest hair as he carried her over to the bed.

He laid her down gently and resolved in his mind to savor every precious moment with her. Nash positioned himself next to her, propping himself up on an elbow so he could take in the full glory of her.

With his hands, he spread her dark silken hair about her and fingered the strands where they fell about her body. She rose to meet his touch, her eyes flickering shut and her lips parting in a quiet moan. Silently, he traced his finger down her profile, pausing to dip into her parted mouth. Her tongue darted out to meet his fingertip and he groaned at her unknowing invitation. Nash's shaking fingers continued down the delicate arch of her neck before dipping between her breasts and circling around each nipple.

"Nash," she whimpered.

He answered her with a searing kiss and clasped a hand around her breast, scraping his fingers over a hardened nipple. Grace met his kiss, but he pulled back before she could draw him in too deeply. His control was being sorely tested by this angel and he had no wish to push her further than she could manage, as much as his body said otherwise.

Ignoring her sounds of protest, he forced himself back and she soon quietened when he laid kisses upon her damp skin. She writhed underneath him, gasping at each touch of his lips upon her flesh. Nash kissed down her collarbone, lavishing attention on her breasts before moving down, down, brushing over her quivering belly. His fingers finally tracked a path to the juncture of her thighs, and he admired her before stroking across the sweet damp heat that awaited him.

GRACE JOLTED AT his touch, but he placed a large, reassuring hand on her stomach, holding her down before tentatively touching his tongue to her folds.

She jerked as a bolt of sensation rumbled through her, setting her skin alight. "Nash!"

Quickly overcoming her shock, she marveled at the teasingly blissful feeling of his mouth upon her sex and she answered his every move with a thrust of her hips while she coiled her hands into his hair.

Who knew a man's mouth just *there* could do such things?

When she felt she could take no more, Nash slid a finger into her slick heat and she exploded, a cry wresting from her.

A luxurious lethargy cascaded over her and she looked at him with heavy lidded satisfaction. He slowly crawled his way back up to her, his large muscular body covering hers. He was careful not to place his weight upon her, as if afraid he would break her, but she enjoyed the feel of Nash's hard thigh settling between her legs and his solid chest pressed against her sensitive skin.

Grace brushed her hands over his rolling muscles, using her fingers to sketch a path over each individual muscle, as he framed her head with his hands

His expression grew grim.

She frowned. "What is it?"

His throat worked. "I do not wish to hurt you."

Grace knew she should be nervous—she had read enough to understand that the first time could be painful—but her curiosity would not allow her to back out now, not after what had just occurred between them.

She put her hands to his rear.

He settled between her legs, burrowing his head into her hair and kissing her neck. Cautiously, he edged forward while he nipped and sucked her ear. The hard heat of him brushed her folds.

With a hurried thrust, he pushed into her, filling her completely. She cried out at the sudden pain, tears forming as she clenched her eyes shut to block out the discomfort.

He waited, apologized again and again in whispers, brushing the tears from her cheeks.

"Damn it," he muttered.

But the sting dissolved, and she became aware of a budding heat, deep in the pit of her stomach, and the awareness spread.

He pressed a fierce kiss to her lips.

He pushed forward slowly, and Grace intuitively responded to the slight movement with the raising of her hips. He inhaled sharply as the movement brought him in deeper.

"Goodness," she whispered. This was unlike anything she could have imagined. No research could have prepared her for such a sensation.

She mourned the loss of the pressure in her when he pulled back but was immediately gratified once more when he lunged again and her whole body tingled.

She pulled him down to kiss her and his tongue delved into her mouth with the same urgency as his thrusts.

Grace could only whimper as the onslaught took hold. She gripped his shoulders and held on for dear life. All thoughts of notes and logic and reasoning were gone. The pressure built and built as he drove himself into her, until finally he pushed his hands under her buttocks, lifting her so that the depth of his next thrust completely unraveled her, shattering her in every way.

She watched his face crumple when he pulled out and gave way to his own pleasure.

Goodness.

Chapter Seventeen

Grace eased out of bed and tiptoed to the door. She paused briefly to eye Nash as he slept peacefully. What a strange thing it had been to wake up next to a man.

What a strange thing the whole night had been.

Strange and wonderful.

But she needed to leave before he awoke. She could not bear for things to be awkward so she concluded her best bet was to leave.

"Where do you think you are going?"

She froze. "Oh, I am just..." She indicated to the door and took a few steps back. "Um, thank you for last night. It was...um...most excellent."

She twisted and put her hand to the doorknob.

Hands came to her shoulders. He spun her around to face him and before she knew what was happening, his mouth was upon hers, his tongue pressing between her lips.

Grace gasped, her hand coming up to touch him as he used the opportunity to press the kiss deeper, but he grabbed her wrist, pushing it down to her side as he wrapped his arms around her.

All sense seemed to depart her as Nash's body pressed into hers and his tongue invaded her mouth. Her free hand wound up around his neck, stroking at the soft hair that met her fingers before tracing across his jawline.

He twisted her around and hot lips met the crook of her neck and she inhaled sharply as it sent tremors shooting through her. His hands held her own across her body, pushing her into him and she could feel the hard length of his manhood.

"I will not do anything that you do not wish. Say the word and I'll let you go," he whispered before brushing his teeth over her ear and lavishing attention on her neck. "Say it, Grace, and this shall be over."

Grace's head lolled back as her legs trembled beneath her, but Nash kept her upright, his hand snaking around her waist.

She said nothing, biting down on her bottom lip while tingles made every tiny hair on her body stand on end.

With a groan, his hand skimmed upwards, brushing lightly over her breast. She whimpered at the faint touch, her nipples unbearably hard. His other hand settled onto her hip, angling her into him, and she writhed against the solidity that awaited her.

Tilting her head back, she was gratified to feel his lips upon hers once more, this time lingering more carefully. Grace eagerly met his tongue with hers.

He groaned again as she kissed him back with relish and she smiled against his lips. How different she felt in his arms, how strong, how powerful. She had the power to make him groan.

Nash tugged at her chemise and his fingers swept over the stiff peaks that poked from beneath, teasing them until they became impossibly tight.

His other hand crept down to the tender flesh between her legs and, though the briefest dart of panic made her heart race, she quickly gave herself up to his touch. She wanted this, more than anything. She'd weighed up all the possibilities and she'd come to her conclusion.

He kept her clamped to him with the press of his hand on her breast as his fingers brushed at the damp heat of her through her chemise. She sighed as he stroked over the heat, the moisture that awaited him quickly seeping into the fabric of her shift. A growl erupted from him when she ground against his touch, the ache in her sex replaced with a gratifying tingle.

In a sudden flash of movement, both of his hands came about the neckline of her chemise and he ripped it from her as she squealed in shock. Grace instinctively covered herself with her hands, but he was swiftly upon her, peeling her stiff hands away.

"You are beautiful, Grace. In so many ways."

"I'm like a boy," she could not help but whisper.

He cupped her breasts. "These do not belong to a boy." Then he moved his hand down to her waist and spanned it with a hand. "This is most certainly a woman's waist." His hand finally cupped her rear. "And this, Good Lord, is the most perfectly female arse."

The soft fabric of his shirt rubbed against her bare back as he tugged her into him, both hands closing over her breasts. His breath hissed between his teeth as he spread his hands over her soft flesh and Grace trembled.

"You are exquisite," he grated out.

She felt it. She really, really felt it.

He buried his face into her hair as his thumbs continued to rasp over her nipples. A hand left her breast and she felt bereft, longing for the rough heat once more. However, the warmth of his hand was soon back on her skin and trailing over her stomach, carefully snaking toward her sex. Her muscles contracted under the gentle touch which seemed almost uncertain and questioning.

In response, she lifted her hips and he took that as her acceptance, easing his hand to the silken skin that awaited him. A finger dropped very briefly into the damp juncture before swirling over her pulsating core, causing her to buck. He continued tormenting her, keeping her pinioned with one hand to her breast, and she found herself reaching for something, an ending to the torturous but blissful sensations.

Two fingers penetrated her, plunging swiftly, and her eyes widened in the dull lamplight as the ache seemed to both quench and inflame. In and out he went, and she continued to writhe under his attentions as he kissed her tenderly.

He quickened the pace and she struggled to breathe. Nash's thumb brushed over her sensitive nub and she cried out as the fiery heat enveloped her, sending her shuddering with waves of rapture.

Grace lay limply in his grasp, his fingers still imbedded in her, as she tried to gain her breath and gather her senses. Easing himself from her, he turned her to face him.

Nash's mouth came down on hers, tenderly, cautiously, and she reacted similarly, savoring the sweet warmth and the press of his lips. His hands twisted into her hair.

"Lie down," he whispered against her lips.

Grace obeyed, hurrying to the curtained bed. She nearly pulled aside the sheets but decided against it, enjoying the feel of her nudity and forgetting any vulnerability in the dark cloak of the night. Instead she felt mischievous and delightfully shameless.

She stared at the canopy above while he undressed. The desire to look at him warred with her hammering heart and she couldn't be certain how she would react to his nudity so she waited until he moved over to the bed.

Reaching out blindly, she gasped as her hand connected with hard male flesh. She heard the sharp intake of his breath as she explored him, spreading her fingers across the lithe muscles that awaited her touch.

"Goodness," she murmured, taking in the sight of crisp hair and flexing muscles.

Grace continued her exploration downwards, following the trail of rough hair beneath his stomach. The velvety softness of his arousal combined with such power shocked her and she drew back.

Drawing in a breath, she reached out again, this time ready for the feeling of him and she clasped him carefully, delighting in his groan and the instinctive thrust of his hips. Slowly, she moved her hand up and down, guided by the appreciative noises he made.

"Christ, Grace, you're going to kill me." He snatched her wrist, pressing it back against the bed. When his weight came across her, her mind went hazy at the feel of his warm flesh aligned with hers.

He eased her other hand up above her head, leaving her open to exploration. She trembled as his finger traced a path along the tender skin of the underside of her arm.

"That feels quite nice," she murmured.

He smiled against the side of her breast. "This will feel nice too." His tongue flicked out, trailing a path across her skin until he reached her nipple. Pausing to blow across it, he promptly surrounded it with his mouth, the sensation so intense, she arched from the bed.

His other hand came underneath her, holding her body to his mouth. Writhing, she moaned as he flicked from one rosy tip to the other, desperate for her hands to be released so she could clutch him to her.

Finally, he released her hands so that he could kiss her all over, trailing kisses down her stomach, her thighs, her hips. She held her breath and eyed his dark head against her pale skin. She supposed she finally understood the appeal of sex. It was wicked and oh so exciting.

Impatiently, she tugged him back up to her breasts, securing his head against her. "I like it when you touch my nipples."

"I very, very much like touching them."

After lavishing attention on her nipples, he flipped her over, her face thrust into her pillow. Turning her head to the side with a gasp, she sank into the mattress as his muscular body covered hers, his manhood pushing against her bottom.

Nash's lips came to the side of her face and he nibbled on her lobe and breathed into the shell of her ear.

Grace moaned. Who would have thought not being able to see him properly could be so...so erotic?

The moisture from his hot breath registered on the back of her neck and she shivered as his lips danced ever so lightly across the sensitive skin.

"Do you like this?"

She nodded frantically, praying he would do something to end her suffering and bring back some of the delightful sensations.

He moved away briefly but she remained where she was, laid out with her hands above her head and her bottom reaching for his touch. A lone finger followed the curve of her spine, lingering just above the soft flesh of her bottom before his lips shadowed the path, sweeping over her bottom and placing a sound kiss to each cheek.

That teasing finger dipped between her cheeks, toying ever so lightly in the slippery softness that begged for his touch. She muffled her squeal of exasperation by burying her head into her pillow as her bottom intuitively lifted to his touch. His fingers plunged suddenly inside her, startling her, before withdrawing and leaving her bereft.

The heat of his body covered hers suddenly and he lifted her hips off the bed slightly, the tip of his cock meeting the folds of her sex, and Grace realized this was it. He was going to take her now.

"From behind?" she asked, unsure if her voice shook from desire or trepidation.

"It will feel deep for you," he said, and she heard a smile in his voice. "You should enjoy it."

Nash moved hesitantly, pressing lightly against her and then retreating.

"Take me," she begged.

He buried himself in her with a groan. "Bloody hell."

Grace could hardly think, hardly breathe. He filled her so completely, so perfectly, it was as if he was made for her. Just when she thought it couldn't get any better, he withdrew, before pumping back in.

He moved easily inside her and she found a rhythm, moving to bring him deeper and deeper. Over and over, he lunged until they were slick with sweat and Grace could do little other than shudder with pleasure as each thrust brought her closer and closer to the edge.

"I need to..." He stopped suddenly, withdrawing and putting a hand under her hip so he could turn her to face him.

Before she could ask him what he wanted, his mouth descended upon hers with a frantic, passionate kiss and he grabbed her thighs, wrapping her legs about him as he joined with her once more.

Grace kissed him deeply, digging her fingernails into the rolling muscles of his back. She threw her head back and took every hard thrust. How it felt so natural already, she could not fathom but could not help wonder what other ways there were of making love.

And would he show them to her?

Bucking her hips against him, she sucked in harsh breaths as her body tingled. The bed squeaked beneath her and the frame thudded against the wall. She closed her eyes, pressed her forehead against his chest, and held her breath when the pleasure broke, splintering through her.

She opened her eyes to watch Nash thrust several more times before withdrawing and spilling himself over her thighs.

He pressed his forehead to hers. "Ah, Grace, do you have to stare at a man with those wide eyes? It's enough to make a man paranoid."

"But it's so fascinating."

"Something like that."

She glanced at the clock on the mantelpiece. "Do you think we have time for...more?"

He chuckled and turned then reached for a cloth to clean her up. She could not help but stare at his rear.

"Let us rest a little while," he said while he dabbed her thighs. "Something you will learn about men is that we do need a small amount of time to recover."

She nodded and smiled. "I am learning a lot today."

"Not to worry. I have lots, lots more to teach you."

Chapter Eighteen

"Bollocks," Nash hissed.

Mary's gaze skipped between the two of them, a brow raised. Nash sat up, using his body as a shield for Grace.

Not that Grace seemed bothered at all by being discovered in his bed. She curled a hand around his arm and peered around him. "We've been found?"

Mary shook her head. "Not yet but my brother said someone was asking about you in the Eight Bells. Or a woman of your description."

Nash cursed again. How the hell had anyone tracked them so closely? Russell was about the most cautious kidnapper anyone could get. All he could think was that something had happened with the ransom to give them away. He rubbed a hand over his face.

That did not feel right either. Russell and Guy were too smart for that.

"We need to leave," he announced.

Grace banded the bedsheet around her and nodded.

He'd half-expected her to argue but either she trusted him to a fault or she had already worked it out in that far-too-logical mind of hers that staying was too dangerous, and if someone was hunting them, it would not take long for them to figure out they could be in the abandoned old house.

"Mary, can you gather Grace's gowns and a change of clothes for me? We'll have to go on foot."

Mary nodded. "Of course."

"I'll write a letter to Russell and Guy, let them know what's happening. Can you ensure it is sent?"

She nodded again and hastened out of the room. Nash turned to Grace and curved a hand around her face. "I will not let anything happen to you, I swear."

Eyes wide, she clasped a hand over his. "You're strong and clever. I am certain you will not."

"Woman, you certainly do know how to compliment a man."

"It wasn't a compliment, merely an observation."

He chuckled and pressed a kiss to her forehead. "Get dressed, with haste. We will leave within the hour."

She slipped her chemise over her head and he closed his eyes briefly. This was not at all how he intended to start the day. He'd rather have had more time to explore her body, taste every inch of her. Even a whole night of lovemaking wasn't enough to fulfill his need for her.

Instead they would have to make a run for it.

He wasn't scared, at least not for him. He could protect her easily enough and he'd go through hell and back to ensure she didn't have to marry that bastard Worthington, but there could be a whole crowd of paid men hunting her and he wasn't willing to put his life on the line unless he could guarantee her safety. It would be far better to get some distance and join forces with Guy and Russell at the lake house. Her safety was not something he was willing to wager on.

Thank the Lord, they had a backup plan. They had never had to use it before, but cautious Guy had made it clear what should be done should something go awry. Mostly it involved getting the hell out of the house but at least he didn't have to think about where they would go.

After dressing swiftly, he splashed cold water over his face and ignored the crumpled sheets on his bed that still smelled of Grace. It was hard to have any regrets, especially when she had made such a sound argument, but he had broken his vow to Guy and Russell. Maybe that would mean this whole Kidnap Club thing was over for him and maybe that meant his strict idea of sticking to promises had bent a little, but he'd be damned if he could regret being Grace's first.

God damn, though, he'd love to be her last too. Never in his life had he had a possessive thought over a woman, but he did now. Several of them in fact.

He shook his head and pushed his feet into his boots then hurried downstairs to pen a hasty letter to Guy. With any luck, it would reach him in a day with the help of a fast messenger and he would have the extra muscle needed to protect Grace. He wasn't proud. He was strong and capable and an excellent shot too. But if he had to ask every man in England to keep her safe, he would.

Curses, he had better retrieve his pistol too. He rose from the writing desk and found Mary in the entranceway, two bags in hand.

"I think you have all you need," she said.

He handed her the letter. "As fast as possible if you can. And once we are gone, can you close up and ensure you're not seen? I wouldn't have you getting into trouble."

Mary grinned. "I think I have enough protection with my brothers."

Nash considered the three burly men and nodded. "That is true."

"How do you think they found us?"

He shrugged. "Lord knows. Hopefully Russell can answer that. He might know something I don't, and the man has a brain almost bigger than Grace's."

Her brows rose.

"It's true. He might seem the quiet, brutish sort but I've seen him read through books in under an hour and he's forever quoting Shakespeare."

"Well, I hope you can keep Grace safe." Mary's smile turned impish. "And at your side."

"You saw nothing."

"Of course I didn't but if it helps, I think she's perfect for you."

Oh great. The last thing he needed was Mary rooting for some sort of future for them. Grace still did not know the full extent of his past and while they might be ridiculously compatible in bed, it did not mean they could carve out a future together.

"She's perfect," he agreed. "Just not for me."

"YOU CAN'T BRING the cat."

Grace clutched the basket handle closer to her body. "I am not leaving Claude behind. Mary said she has been instructed to keep clear of the house. Who will look after him?"

Nash groaned. "Can't he eat mice or something? We will come back to collect him once you are safe, I promise."

She eyed him. Apparently bedding a man did not make him understand one any more than previously. Or had he bed her?

She was just not certain. After all, she had been the one to ask him to make love to her, but Nash had most certainly taken the lead.

And what a lead it was...

She shook her head. Now was not the time to be thinking of last night. The most logical thing to do was set it aside for the time being and worry about it later. Anytime now, whoever her uncle had sent to track her down could come across them, and if he had sent more than one man, they could certainly be in danger.

The strangest thing was, she couldn't quite bring herself to be frightened. Not yet anyway. Maybe this was what lovemaking did to one—created this strange, fuzzy, warm sensation that would not dissipate even in the face of great danger. No wonder men and women in love so often made such disastrous decisions.

Not that she would. She lifted her chin and faced Nash down. He might have made her feel things she never thought possible last night but there was no chance she was leaving Claude to fend for himself whilst they fled.

He sighed. "Fine." He offered out a hand. "Give me the basket."

She hesitated a moment then handed over the basket holding the cat. Claude gave a little meow of annoyance at his confined state, but they did not have much choice.

Nash grimaced. "I hope he doesn't make a racket the whole journey. We need to be surreptitious."

"Claude knows how to be surreptitious."

A dark brow rose, and his lips tilted a little. "Indeed." He tugged his pocket watch out of his waistcoat and flicked it open.

"We need to get moving." He shoved it back into his pocket. "If we make haste, we can reach the inn just after sunset."

"Where precisely are we going?"

"An inn."

"Yes, but where?"

"Far from here."

"I think I should know where."

"Fine. The Royal Oak in White Moss."

She wrinkled her nose. "I don't know of a White Moss."

"Precisely." He reached for her hand. "Now, can we please get moving?"

She took his hand, his fingers enfolding hers. She eyed the contrast between his dark gloves and her pale blue ones. How odd it was that they had been touching, skin to skin, not so long ago, yet the simple act of him holding her hand made her stomach twirl. How aggravating it was that they were having to flee, and she would have no time to write any notes of last night or think over the act of lovemaking fully.

"We will head up over the hill and avoid the village entirely," he explained as they followed a faintly worn path through the grass.

"How did someone find us?"

"I'll be damned if I know. No one apart from Mary and a handful of others know of our presence here. I'm always careful to arrive here quietly, as is Russell. Most people still think the place is abandoned."

"Would one of Mary's brothers give us away?"

He shook his head. "They don't know what she does. Besides, they're good men and Mary would have their heads if they did."

"The boy then?"

"He's paid well to keep quiet." He scowled. "It would be a damned shame if someone has betrayed us."

"Why are we going to this inn, specifically?"

He came to a stop at the ridge of the hill. Gray clouds hung like lead over the fields, casting the grass in a dull light. Grace only hoped the rain stayed away long enough for them to reach wherever White Moss was. Claude would not be happy about sitting in a wet basket.

"We have a backup plan."

"We?"

"The Kidnap Club," he explained. "We've never had to use it before, but should we be discovered, it was always planned that we decamp to that inn."

"And then what?"

"Grace, as much as I love your inquisitive mind, sometimes I wish you would let a man just be a man and take charge."

"I do not see how asking questions is not letting you take charge. Sometimes a woman should like to know exactly where she might be going before blindly following a man."

He closed his eyes briefly. "You are right, of course. I'm simply trying to get us there as quickly as possible and I need to ensure you are safe."

The concern in his eyes made her heart jolt—and not in a good way. Somehow, she had forgotten the risk they were all taking in this act. Should her uncle find her, she would be forced to marry a murderer and Nash could be charged with kidnapping.

"I understand."

He started moving again and she followed along. "We will head to a house in Derbyshire. Guy has it let under some secret name, just in case."

"Derbyshire? That's some distance."

He turned and grinned. "Not to worry, we will not walk all the way. With any luck, the cavalry shall be turning up to assist before long."

Chapter Nineteen

The sound of Grace's teeth chattering set Nash's own teeth on edge. Damn this whole thing to hell. How could someone have found them? He had been trying his best all day to remain calm and not snap but the mere fact someone had come so close to discovering Grace made him want to thrust his fist through the window he was currently staring out of.

Rain splattered the glass pane, offering little more than a view of glistening darkness. The weather had finally unleashed on them at least two miles from the inn and they were both drenched to the skin. He turned to eye Grace, bundled up under a blanket on a chair by the fire. Hair plastered to pale skin, her tiny frame was swamped in the thick knitted blanket.

Her teeth continued to chatter.

He strode over and kneeled in front of her, putting hands to her arms and rubbing vigorously. "You'll warm up soon," he assured her.

She had to. If she sickened because of him, he'd never forgive himself. Someone as small as Grace was likely to fall ill easily, surely? He should have demanded a cart from a farmer on route or commandeered a vehicle somewhere. To hell with the plan. Just because Guy said should something go wrong, they would have to avoid being seen by anyone didn't mean Nash had to obey him.

"W-what do we do now?" she asked.

"We get you warm first." He glanced at the door. "We should have hot food and drink shortly, that will help."

Nash had signed them in as husband and wife, so they were sharing a room. Far better that she be at his side and he hoped no one would pay much attention to a married couple. Neither of them drew much attention, being soaked to the skin and looking nothing like a nobleman and an heiress, and they'd keep to the room until he heard from Guy or Russell.

Thankfully, the room was well-appointed, tucked under the eaves of the inn with an antechamber and clean linens. Guy had good taste in traveler's inns at least.

"T-then what?" she pressed.

"We wait."

"To go to Derbyshire?"

He nodded. "The plan is that someone will arrive with a carriage—most likely Russell—and we'll travel from here to the house."

"I-I'm glad you have a good plan."

"I will keep you safe," he vowed.

"I know."

A knock at the door drew him to his feet. He opened it and took the tray of steaming food and tea from the serving girl with a brief thank you. After setting the tray on the table in front of the fire, he poured Grace a cup of tea and added sugar and milk, just how he knew she liked it. She cupped the drink gratefully in her hands and inhaled deeply.

"I feel better already."

"Good." He poured a tea for himself then set out the bowls of stew. His stomach grumbled. No wonder as they hadn't eaten all day and he was functioning on little energy after being, er, preoccupied all night. He waited until Grace had finished her drink, however, before digging in, gobbling down the tender meat and large chunks of vegetables. Grace followed suit and they ate in silence until their bowls were empty.

"Do you feel better?"

She nodded. "Much better, thank you." She looked over to where the cat had settled on the bed. "Looks like Claude has forgiven us for the basket too."

"He's a placid cat, despite everything," he agreed.

"He is." She tilted her head. "Even when I found him, all bedraggled and starving, he was the most relaxed cat I ever met."

"He's not a bad chap, I suppose."

She smiled. "Admit it, you are beginning to like him. I saw you giving him fish the other day."

He lifted a shoulder. "I tolerate him, that is all. And the fish was only going to go to waste."

"If you say so."

He rose from his seat. "We should get you out of that dress. We can get it cleaned and dried then."

Her eyes widened. "I only have a shift on underneath."

"Need I remind you that I saw you in significantly less than that last night."

Her cheeks pinkened. "Well, yes, but that was...different."

"How?"

"I don't know, it just was."

He sighed. This whole mess had ruined everything. If it weren't for being discovered, he'd have taken her to bed again tonight and found other ways of making her cry out and sigh with contentment.

Even if it meant he was probably going to be condemned to hell for taking her virginity and breaking his promise.

It would be worth every agonizing moment, he was certain of it.

"If I turn around, will you take it off? You can wrap yourself back up in the blanket and be perfectly decent."

"That would work, I suppose."

He turned and listened to the rustle of clothing. It was wrong. *He* should be the one removing that gown from her, peeling it away from her skin then shoving her shift down her shoulder so he could nibble on her collarbone. Then he would go down...down...

Bloody hell, he was not helping himself here.

He focused on the ugly crisscross pattern of the blanket on the bed and breathed deeply. He was calm. Placid. He did not wish to kill the fiancé and uncle who had forced them on the run. He did not want to turn around and take her in a deep kiss. He would not give away any of his frustration at this situation.

Entirely, perfectly calm.

She had to be done by now, surely? He turned around and she yelped, covering herself with a blanket.

Nipples. A little bit of shoulder.

Far, far, far from calm.

IT WAS NOT that the flash of desire in his eyes went unnoticed. She appreciated it too. Here she was with damp hair and likely looking like a frail street urchin and he still desired her.

She still desired him. Glancing at his strong back, shaped by the dampness of his shirt, she recalled feeling the rippling muscles there, digging her fingers into his skin while he gave her pleasurable moment after pleasurable moment.

However, it didn't seem appropriate to act upon it whilst they were in danger nor could she feel that same sense of boldness she had possessed the previous night.

She bunched the blanket tighter around her shoulders and hauled the sleeves off her chemise from where they had fallen. Maybe it was because being with Nash had not felt like mere coupling or some biological act. She had not just felt things, she had *felt* things. Deep inside her, he'd triggered something and for the first time ever, she had no longer been able to think. He'd swept her away last night and she feared she might not return should they make love again.

"You can turn around now."

He turned slowly then relaxed his shoulders when he saw her covered state. She handed him the damp gown and waited by the fire until he returned from delivering it to a laundry maid. He nodded toward the bed when he returned. "You can rest if you want. It's been a long day."

She shook her head. Physically she was tired, but her mind would not settle, of that she was certain. Not only did she have to contemplate all that had happened between them, but she had her uncle or whoever these men were to worry about.

Nash shrugged and went over to the window, then turned and paced past. She counted each time he paced, paused to look out of the window, then paced again. She doubted there was much to see. The window faced the rear of the building where no light from the stables or the lanterns could be seen. Ten times he did it before she spoke up.

"Nash, you need not fret. I trust you will keep us safe."

He paused, unclenched his fists, and came to sit opposite her. "There's no chance they could track us here. It is not even on the main road."

"Precisely."

"We won't be here long anyway, with any luck."

"Exactly."

"And who would think to look for you in Derbyshire?"

"No one."

He shook his head, a half-smile stretched across his lips. "Am I not meant to be the one reassuring you?"

"You already have."

He peered at her. "I thought you would be terrified."

"I thought I would too, but I feel safe with you." She gestured to him. "Why would I not? You are strong and capable and quite the determined man."

He released a soft chuckle. "You mentioned the strong bit before, but I think a few people would argue with the capable and determined part."

She scowled. "Like who?"

He waved a hand. "It does not matter."

"Who, Nash?" she pressed.

He blew out a breath. "My father mostly, I suppose."

"He thinks you incapable?"

"Incapable, foolish, careless, and most certainly not determined, unless one counts determined to mess my life up royally."

"What happened to make him think that of you?"

"It's a long story."

"We have time."

He rubbed a hand over his jaw. "Let us just say I was a wild sort of a man after Cambridge. My father did not appreciate it much."

She nodded, remaining silent. She just knew there was more to his past and she wanted all the story but feared asking too much in case he ceased talking.

"He disowned me when I turned four and twenty," he muttered. "I have not seen him or the rest of my family since then."

So that explained his lack of funds. "I am sorry, that must be difficult."

He summoned a grin. "Well, it could be worse. At least I have a father. I cannot complain when you have suffered so at the hands of your uncle without your father to protect you."

"I loved my father dearly and he was the kindest of men," she admitted. "My mother died trying to birth my brother, who died with her, so it was just the two of us. He doted on me wonderfully." She paused. "I cannot help but wonder if he doted too much. I went everywhere with him and there was nothing we did not discuss, even when I was a young child. He thought it important that a girl's mind be fully shaped before she became a woman. I feel like maybe I knew too much of the world."

And she knew to fear it so early on.

"He sounds an interesting man, simply trying to do his best to raise a daughter. There are many fathers who would have little to do with their daughters."

"Like your father?"

"Actually, no. My father is a kindly person and treated my sisters well indeed."

"But he disinherited you."

"Yes."

"Nash, what happened that he might make such a decision if he is indeed a kindly man?"

He shook his head. "The past is in the past." He rose from his chair. "Little point in discussing it. Now shall we get some rest?"

She glanced at the empty bed where Claude had curled up at the end. "Will you...will you share it with me?"

"If that is what you wish."

Grace debated it for a moment. There were things she still did not know about this man and her mind did not want to let go of that fact. Her father would have told her to look at everything she knew and weigh it up carefully before throwing herself into the moment. But right now, her instincts told her she wanted him next to her, his body touching hers, his arms wrapped around her, even if just to sleep.

She nodded and his posture relaxed a little. Who would have thought she would have the power to unnerve such a man? It was rather a heady feeling.

Chapter Twenty

"Stay hidden," Nash ordered Grace at the sound of knocking on the door to their room. It could be Russell, but he wasn't taking any chances.

He inched the door open and the inn's serving girl peered through the crack. He opened it farther and glanced down the hallway.

"Forgive the disturbance, sir, but you asked me to inform you should anyone be looking for a man and a woman travelling together."

"Yes?"

"They are downstairs now. Four men."

Nash slipped a coin shilling into her hand. "Thank you. If you would be so good as to keep our presence silent, that would be much appreciated."

She nodded. "We never give away any details of our guests, sir. We're a good establishment."

"That you are, please convey my thanks to the owner."

He closed the door and turned toward Grace. Curled up in the chair by the fire, she had a book she found in her lap and was twirling a dark strand of hair around one finger. Lord, he hated having to do this again to her but there was no time to waste. Simply because the serving girl wouldn't say anything didn't mean anyone else could not be bribed with coin.

"Grace, we need to leave. Now."

Her eyes widened. "What has happened?"

"There are people here, likely looking for us. I would not want to gamble on them finding us." He snatched up his jacket and shoved his arms into it. "Four men, so I am outnumbered."

She nodded vigorously and stood, hastily slipping on her shoes and snatching up Claude. He made a startled noise when she pushed him into the basket and his claws could be heard scrabbling at the wicker.

Nash took the basket from her, grabbed their bags, and did a quick scan of the room. No sign of their stay here which was excellent. Now they just had to escape unnoticed.

"We'll go out of the stable door," he said. "If they're in the tap room, asking questions, we can avoid being spotted."

He eased open the door again, checked that the hallway remained empty, and led the way downstairs. His heart thudded hard in his chest and his palms grew clammy around the wicker handle. Chatter and the clanking of plates and cutlery emanated from the taproom door. All it would take was for one of them to open the door and spot them both. Nash regretted not taking the time to load his pistol. If he took one of the men out, then he'd have better chances of taking the rest on.

He didn't need to see them to know they'd be a rough sort. The kind who would chase down anyone for coin, be it criminal or an innocent like Grace. They wouldn't use kind methods either. So he had to make sure they did not lay a finger on her.

Holding his breath, he led the way to the rear of the building, checking behind them sporadically. He stopped at the rear door and inched it open with his shoulder. Not even a stable hand, luckily. He shoved open the door and nodded his head for Grace to follow. They stumbled out into the muddy courtyard.

Several new horses were in the stalls—strong-looking beasts with fine coats. Not the sort to belong to just any man. Whoever it was tracking them, they had funds.

That did not make Nash feel any better.

Voices came from the inn and his gut twisted. "Hide, quick," he hissed, urging Grace to duck down behind an empty stall door. He followed her, crouching in the stale straw. Her eyes were wide, her skin pale. He heard her rapid, unsteady breaths. Nash pressed a finger to his lips as the voices grew closer.

"Could have been them," murmured a man.

"Could have been anyone. What if the boy was wrong?"

"It is them. I know it," said a third man, his voice deep but slightly croaky, as though he were older than the others.

Beside him, Grace stiffened.

"Search the stables. They said the pair had eaten their morning meal here. They cannot have gone far," ordered the older man, with a sigh. "Let's hope this little bitch is worth all this effort."

Grace released a whimper and Claude scuffled in his basket in response to his mistresses' distress. Nash drew out his gun. It might not be ready to fire but it looked threatening enough. If he could hold them off for long enough, he'd tell Grace to run. Squelching footsteps neared and blood pounded in his ears. He pressed himself tight against the door and put a hand to Grace's back, urging her to do the same. A shadow cast itself on the straw behind him then retreated. He held his breath for several moments until the footsteps faded and a door slammed shut.

Slowly, he eased up and peered over the door. The stables were empty once more, so he finally let himself breathe.

"They're gone," he said, standing.

Grace remained hunched where she was, arms wrapped about herself. Her body trembled.

"All is well," he assured her, offering a hand. "They have gone inside."

She shook her head. "It is not well at all." She glanced up at him. "That was my fiancé."

Chapter Twenty-One

Grace would have screamed had she had any energy left when the huge, black carriage swept in front of them, blocking their path. She might have even summoned enough energy for it too had Nash not wrapped a comforting arm around her.

"Not to worry," he said. "That's our ride."

Her legs nearly gave out from underneath her. Thank goodness for his support or she might have ended up a crumpled heap on the muddy ground. She squinted at the two men atop the closed carriage, their features shadowed and hidden.

"We were nearly discovered," Nash explained to them as he pulled open the door and ushered Grace inside.

"Get in," one of the men said and she realized it was Russell, the man who had brought her to Nash.

She sank gratefully into the plush interior of the carriage, leaning her head back against the wood and closing her eyes. She should have known a man like Worthington would seek his quarry himself. And those men with him...A shiver trailed through her. They had sounded strong and terrifying.

As much as she trusted Nash to do whatever he could to protect her, he could have been hurt had they been discovered—or worse. After all, he was her kidnapper. It would be a hard thing to explain to a judge that she had been willingly taken and in the court's eyes she was still her uncle's property.

She opened her eyes and wrapped her arms about herself. Her heart thudded rapidly, echoing in her ears and making her breaths seem loud. That had been far, far too close.

Nash climbed inside and slammed the door shut. He had barely seated himself next to her before they set off at a vicious pace. She might have been scared about travelling so fast on country road in the dark but the farther away they were from the inn—and Mr. Worthington—the better.

"That was too damned close," Nash muttered, leaning his head back.

She could only nod.

He straightened and twisted toward her. "Forgive me, Grace. I should have been more cautious." He shook his head and made a disgusted sound. "Lord knows how they tracked us there."

"You were hardly reckless." She wrapped her arms tighter about herself when her teeth began to chatter.

He cursed softly and snatched up a blanket from the opposite side of the carriage then tucked it about her.

"I-I am not cold," she protested.

"No, you are scared, but this will help." He tucked her up and she sank gratefully into the blanket. He eased an arm around her shoulders, and she leaned into him. It didn't take long for her teeth to stop chattering or the knots in her stomach to unwind once pressed against him.

"Mr. Worthington is a determined man," she commented.

"So it seems," he said tightly.

She glanced up at him, just able to make out the firm line of his jaw in the dim light of the lanterns from outside. "We are safe from him now."

"Yes."

She lifted away a little and pressed a hand to his chest. "Nash, all is well."

He gave a half-smile. "I'm comforting you, remember?"

"Perhaps we can comfort each other?"

"Perhaps." He drew her back into him, and she rested her head against his shoulder.

She didn't recall falling asleep but when she woke, Nash was still awake, and the dull light of morning lit the interior of the vehicle. She peered at the inside of the carriage, flicking her gaze from the luxurious cushions to the silk padded interior. This was no normal carriage. Whoever it belonged to had to be wealthy indeed.

She yawned and stretched. "Where are we?"

"About fifteen miles from the house."

"I hope it is far enough away."

"If they track us there, I'd think they were clairvoyant."

She wrinkled her nose. "There is no such thing as clairvoyant."

"Many people would disagree with you."

"I have yet to see any real evidence they exist," she said firmly.

He chuckled. "I am not going to argue with you over the existence of the paranormal right now, Grace."

"Well, it would not be an argument. There is no scientific proof for such things."

He shook his head. "Do you ever switch that mind of yours off?"

She frowned. "Maybe?"

"Well, at least you got some rest."

"Did you?"

He shrugged. "A little."

She doubted it. His eyes were a little red and ringed with dark circles. Stubble had appeared on his chin overnight and it reminded her of when she had awoken in his arms and felt the rough texture against her bare skin.

Goodness, what was wrong with her? Picturing such things when they were on the run? Yet she could not help reaching out and smoothing a hand along his jaw, recalling how powerful and wonderful she had felt when he had been spreading kisses across her body as though he were worshipping her.

"What was that for?" he asked.

"Thank you for everything, Nash."

"You forget I am just doing my job."

"I do not think every man who is paid to do their job does it quite so diligently as you."

He leaned down and brushed a brief kiss across her lips. "If I was diligent, we would never have been discovered."

"You cannot blame yourself for that. It is likely they were checking all inns along the road."

"But how could they even know we took that road?"

"Perhaps Worthington has a lot of men searching. It was just a coincidence he happened to be searching ours."

"I know you do not believe in coincidences any more than I do," he said tightly.

Grace blew out a breath. She did not. And, unfortunately, that meant they might have a turncoat in their midst.

NASH HAD LITTLE desire to make Grace any more terrified than she already was, but he was struggling to fight his emotions. He forced himself to unfurl his fists. He'd always considered himself a fairly relaxed person. The only time he'd ever lost his temper was when his father had announced he was cutting him off. But seeing her fiancé for himself...he blew out a heated breath. If Grace had not been there, Nash would have pounced on him and beaten him to a pulp, regardless of being outnumbered.

It didn't help Grace was clever. She understood full well someone had betrayed them. There were so few of them involved that it was hard to fathom who. He trusted everyone who assisted them or else they would never be involved. His only fear was someone had been threatened. He prayed to God Mary was well.

Even when they stopped in the late afternoon, he was unable to rid himself of his anger. He kept glancing at Grace with her wide eyes and fragile form and picturing her marrying Worthington. His jaw hurt from grinding his teeth. He must have given himself away as Guy put a hand to his shoulder and tugged him aside as Russell helped Grace from the carriage.

"She'll be safe here. We don't have much longer left and we will stay to help you protect her."

Nash nodded. It wouldn't hurt to have Guy and Russell's muscles, especially as Worthington's hired brutes were likely no stranger to fighting dirty and wouldn't think twice about harming Grace so long as they got paid.

Russell lifted the basket holding Claude and eased open the lid. The cat let out a plaintive wail and Russell snapped the basket shut. "That animal gets uglier by the day," he muttered to Nash.

"He's not so bad." Nash took the basket from Russell who shook his head with a grin.

"What are we doing now?" Grace asked, smoothing hands down her crumpled gown.

"We'll walk to the house. It's a few miles but an easy enough walk," Nash explained.

"And we'll take the carriage to an inn. Keep it out of sight and ensure there are no tracks to the house," said Guy.

Her eyes widened. "You do not think they could follow our tracks, do you?"

"Not at all." Russell climbed back into the driver's seat. "But we like to be cautious."

"We'll be back after dark," Guy said to Nash.

Grace watched the carriage leave and she turned to him, mouth open. "I just realized..."

"Yes?"

"That's the Earl of Henleigh's carriage." She pinched the bridge of her nose. "I recognized the crest from a book of lineage."

"It is indeed," Nash said with a smile.

"He's the one behind this?"

Nash simply grinned.

"Oh Lord, one of them was the earl? Or do not tell me you stole it from the earl?" She put hands to her cheeks. "No, *you're* not the earl, are you?"

He shook his head with a chuckle. "I am no earl. But Guy is Lord Guy Huntingdon, Earl of Henleigh. He's the one that started The Kidnap Club." He nodded along the path that wove along the hillside. "Come, we had better get moving."

"I cannot believe I didn't realize."

"Guy doesn't stand upon ceremony much so I wouldn't worry."

"How exactly did he start this?" she asked, falling in step beside him.

Nash peered out over the hills. There was no sign of the cottage yet, but he'd been forced to memorize this path just in case and once they were over the next hill, it would be ahead of them—a white painted thing nestled just by a large lake.

"Guy's cousin was in a terrible marriage. Her husband beat her to within an inch of her life and he refused to give her up in any way, shape or form. So Guy helped her escape to America but first she was 'kidnapped' and ransomed so the husband would not try to chase her down. She's settled happily in America with her little girl now and the husband drank himself to death eventually."

"Goodness."

"This was before I was involved but the cousin told another woman of what Guy had done for her and it sort of spread from there. That's when he brought us on board."

"Why did you join?"

"I needed the money mostly and it seemed an interesting way to stay occupied. I've known Guy since our college years, and he knew I had the house and the time to look after women under our care."

"It must feel nice to help women in need."

He paused. It had always been about the money for him. At least he thought it had been. Of course he cared about the women he looked after—he hoped for the best for them and was glad they could escape whatever it was they needed to. But he had never thought of it as anything more than a paid job.

Until kidnapping Grace.

Until seeing the bastard of a man she could have been married to. Now he wished he could help more women escape.

"I think the three of you are very brave," she declared.

He shook his head. "Bravery has little to do with it. In truth, I have never thought of it as a very dangerous occupation. Russell takes most of the physical risk and Guy could lose the trust of every single one of his peers if it was found he was helping wives escape."

"They are your peers too, are they not?"

"Not so much these days. Not when one does not have coin. I doubt I pass the thought of a single one of them."

She smiled and took his hand. "Well, that is most certainly their loss."

Nash wasn't so sure.

Chapter Twenty-Two

"Bloody hell, who thought it was a good idea to let this cottage?" Russell shoved a hand through his damp hair and ran it over his face, swiping away the raindrops.

Guy hauled off his soaking wet coat and draped it over the chair in front of the fire and lifted a brow. "You know full well it was mine."

"Couldn't you have found somewhere that did not involve traipsing miles in the dark?" Russell muttered.

Nash poured brandy into three glasses and offered it out. The weather had taken a nasty turn just after he and Grace had arrived at the house. Thankfully there was plenty of dry wood in the stores and he was able to get several fires going.

Guy sank onto a chair. "That was the whole point in having this place," he pointed out. "It is in the middle of nowhere."

"I'm certain there are places in the middle of nowhere with decent paths."

Nash glanced at Russell's mud caked boots as he tugged them off and set them in front of the fire. "I don't suppose I need to ask if you were followed."

"Only an idiot would follow us," Russell grumbled.

"Or someone very determined," Nash reminded them.

He waited until Russell was seated in front of the fire and hauled up a wooden chair to sit beside both men. He cradled the brandy in one hand, swirled the liquid about the glass, and watched it coat the inside.

"You needn't worry," Guy said. "We were cautious, and no one saw us leave the inn. We paid the innkeeper generously to keep the carriage well-hidden too."

"This is the first time we have ever needed to use this house," Nash said. "We were arrogant enough to believe we were safe at my house. I do not want to be so arrogant as to believe it again."

Russell eyed Nash. "Since when were you so serious?"

"Since Grace nearly got snatched out from under my nose."

Russell made a noise. "Like you would let that happen."

"It was too close for my liking." Nash threw back the glass of brandy.

"Fine job I made sure we were fully stocked," Guy said, nodding to the empty glass.

Nash nodded. "We have enough firewood to keep us warm until we need to leave, by the looks of it."

"And Russell and I brought some food supplies." Guy pointed at the ceiling. "I take it Miss Beaumont is resting."

"She did well but I think the shock of it all has taken its toll. She fell asleep almost instantly."

"We should keep watch," Russell suggested. "Won't hurt to be cautious."

"I'll take first watch," Nash volunteered.

Guy shook his head. "You'll rest too."

"You two walked farther than I did, and I'd wager you were travelling longer than me too."

Russell shared a look with Guy. "But you have been watching over her for some time. And you look like death."

Nash straightened in his chair. Every part of him ached as though he had just taken a beating at fencing and his eyes were gritty, his mouth dry. However, he couldn't picture himself being able to close his eyes and rest, not when Grace's fiancé was still out there, hunting them. "I look a darn sight better than you do, my friend."

"I don't think you've had the luxury of a mirror or else you would not be saying that," Russell scoffed.

"I'll take first watch," Guy snapped. "You can both get some rest."

"I don't need rest," Nash protested.

"I want both of you in full health and you would want that too if you desire to keep that woman safe." Guy leaned forward and peered into the fire. "We came too close today to all of this unravelling. If it comes out that we have been aiding other women, they could all end up in danger."

"Not to mention, I'd look terrible with a noose around my neck," muttered Nash.

Russell shook his head. "You two would likely be saved from the noose by way of your rich blood."

Nash snorted. "I am certain my family wouldn't give two hoots. But I don't much fancy finding out."

"After this is over, we go quiet for a while, and we rethink how we do this." Guy shook his head. "We must have lost someone's loyalty."

Russell scowled. "I cannot think of anyone who would betray us."

"Nor can I but how else would we have been tracked?"

Nash curled a fist. "When I get my hands on them..."

"I'll join you," Russell said.

Guy held up a hand. "Worry about how we'll protect Miss Beaumont first. Then we'll worry about who has given us away."

Nash stiffened. "Do you really think I have been worrying about anything else?"

Russell twisted his head to eye him. "You're being awfully uptight about this woman, Nash."

"He is," Guy agreed.

"Can you blame me?" He gestured with his fingers. "We were this close to her being caught."

Russell cocked his head. "I think there's more to it than that."

"There is," Guy agreed.

"Damn it, you two don't know what you're talking about."

"See?" Russell said to Guy. "When was the last time you ever saw him so defensive? I knew something was different the moment I handed her over to him."

"He's definitely changed." Guy finished off the brandy and set the glass on the small table next to his chair. "Don't tell me you finally gave in to temptation."

"Temptation?" Nash spluttered. "What do you take me for?"

Guy shrugged. "A rake."

He couldn't argue with that. He certainly had been. But he had never, ever touched any of the vulnerable women in their care.

Until now.

"Something has happened between you," Russell said. "I can tell." He narrowed his gaze at him.

"It better not have done." Guy clenched his jaw.

Nash opened his mouth then closed it, fighting through the mess that was his mind for some kind of denial.

A feminine squeal smashed through his thoughts and his heart leapt against this chest. All three of them shot to their feet as a bundle of fur ripped into the room and scrabbled up the arm of Guy's chair and Grace dashed into the room in nothing more than her chemise. She froze in front of them, her eyes wide.

"Oh. Um. Good evening."

GRACE COULD NOT decide if the parlor room of the cottage was particularly small or if the three men staring at her were especially big. She suspected she could do some calculations and figure it out, but it would involve measuring them and that wouldn't be especially appropriate.

Not that it would make this situation any more uncomfortable.

They'd been speaking of her. If Claude had not squeezed out of her arms, she might have heard more too. Their conversation was muffled by the half-closed door, but she was certain they'd been quizzing Nash about his relationship with her.

So much of her wanted to speak up and declare that it had been all her fault, that she had demanded he take her to bed, but that would completely give them away then, would it not? Besides, at this point she was not even certain it would happen again.

Stupid. Of course it would not. She was under a week away from her birthday and then she would be free to do whatever she wished with her life. That thought should have made her happy but instead it made her stomach sink. How could she go back to a normal life after being in Nash's arms?

She scurried over and tried to pry Claude off the armchair. The poor creature had suffered a terrible time being trapped in a basket, riding in a carriage, then having to settle in yet another new place. No wonder he'd wanted to escape her room. She never had any intention of eavesdropping and only wanted to take the cat back upstairs, but she couldn't help herself when she'd heard the three men talking.

Of her.

Of her and Nash.

Now she wholly regretted her decision. She should have taken Claude straight upstairs once she'd grabbed him. Even looking at Nash, she was certain she was giving away all the feelings that were threatening to burst out of her chest, as though it were some beacon of light, pulsing away inside her, visible to everyone.

When she looked at him, it was hard to see a collection of features—a handsome jaw, a muscular body, piercing eyes. She saw him as simply Nash—the man who made her feel things that were entirely illogical.

She pulled again on Claude, aware of each man watching her. They were all tall, all strong. The earl had the regal bearing of a nobleman, but he had a slightly weathered look, as though life had done him some grave wrong. Creases were permanently on his brow and gray tinged his sideburns.

Though she had met Russell before, it had all been in such a flurry that she had hardly had time to study him. He was slightly leaner but there was something dangerous behind his tense jaw and steely gaze. Of all the men, he was the most threatening.

Claude finally retracted his claws and she was able to pry him away from the chair and bundle him against her chest. "Sorry," she murmured. "He is feeling a little aggravated."

As were they all, she suspected. She moved through the center of the trio, awareness prickling the hairs on her arms. She really, really regretted trying to eavesdrop now. The masculine aura of the room was enough to make even the boldest of women wish to flee and she was certainly not the boldest. She forced herself to move slowly toward the door rather than scurrying away like a little mouse as she so wished to do. Before she left the room, she offered a cautious smile. "Goodnight."

All three of them eyed her for a moment before jerking into action. Various versions of *goodnight* echoed back.

The earl cleared his throat. "I'll be keeping watch should you need anything."

Grace did not miss Nash glowering at the earl.

Russell nodded. "And Nash and I will be in the room next to yours."

Nash's glower deepened.

"Of course. Goodnight," she repeated. She turned, feeling their gazes upon her back. She stepped out into the hallway and heard hasty footsteps behind her. She didn't dare turn for fear of disappointment until he called her name.

Nash rushed over to her, putting a hand to her arm before she could make her way upstairs. "Grace, I—" He blew out a breath. "I am not certain what you heard but—"

"I was just trying to get Claude," she said, holding up the dejected-looking animal.

"I know but—"

"You should get some sleep. It has been such a long day."

"It has," he agreed.

"I will do the same."

"Grace—" he started again.

"Goodnight, Nash. Rest well."

He glanced at his feet. She wasn't daft. He had more to say but she could not bring herself to hear it. Maybe it was an apology for allowing her to seduce him. Maybe he was going to beg her to keep their liaison quiet. Whatever it was, she could not bear to endure it. The memories of their one night and morning together would stay with her until she was old and gray, of that she was certain, and her heart throbbed painfully at the idea that he might regret it—especially now his friends had them almost figured out.

Or, of course, he wanted to tell her that they were being preposterous. That he could never love someone like her. She knew that but she didn't want to hear it said aloud. They were the least logical couple in existence—she'd known that from the very beginning.

Apparently though, her logical mind refused to function when it came to Nash because the mere mention of the word love had sent her heart fluttering all over the place like a bird trying to fly free.

Well, if she was going to survive the next few days in Nash's company, she would have to keep it locked firmly away.

"Goodnight," he finally said softly and turned away.

Heart lodged firmly in her throat, she headed upstairs, cradling Claude close. "Love is a silly thing," she told the cat in a whisper. "It's only a feeling to ensure men and women wish to procreate."

And she would certainly not be fool enough to think she could feel such a thing for Nash.

Chapter Twenty-Three

"Where is she?" Nash demanded.

Russell paused cleaning his gun. "She is safe, Nash." He shook his head and laid his hands flat on the kitchen table. "Keep worrying like this and you'll end up in an early grave."

"Are you not worried?"

Russell lifted a shoulder. "I've faced danger before."

"Yes, but you are not the one facing it," he pointed out. "She is."

"She seems to be handling it quite well. Many other women would have spent the time weeping and wailing."

Nash couldn't deny Grace was managing this whole 'on the run' scenario terrifically well. She had almost seemed chirpy this morning, so he had to assume she had slept well. The rest of the day, they had avoided each other—or at least he had avoided her. Had she overheard what had been said last night? He had to assume yes by her awkward behavior when he'd spoken with her. Which meant the idea that he might...feel something for her, terrified her.

It terrified him too. Even if Guy hadn't said anything, the inkling was there—this little voice that kept whispering something just out of hearing. Something he had no right to hear. Hell, the woman didn't even known the full truth about him and he couldn't say that he hadn't had the chance to talk to her about it or they were only acquaintances so what was the point, but there had been opportunities, he knew that.

191

And he knew one thing for certain about Grace. She hated greedy men. The way she had spoken of her uncle told him enough. She would hate him for his past too, of that he was certain.

"She's on the balcony," Russell offered. "She asked if there was any paper and a pencil and went up there about an hour ago." Russell rubbed his nose. "Does she like to draw or something?"

Nash shook his head. "She takes notes."

"Notes? What the devil for?"

"I couldn't say. It's just something she seems to do."

Russell shook his head and picked up his gun and cloth. "She's certainly unlike any woman I've ever met."

"That she is," he agreed before heading upstairs.

He stepped through the bedroom to the open doors. The balcony offered a perfect view of the lake at sunset, spread out like an orange splash of paint against darker orange and black hills. The sun spread its fingers of light low across the land, reflected in the water.

Grace had ignored the metal chair in favor of sitting on the floor, her legs curled up beside her whilst she scribbled furiously away on a scrap of paper. He tried to make out some of the words, but her handwriting was a wild mess.

He eased down beside her, but she didn't stop writing so he waited until she had finished before speaking. "It's a beautiful spot." He gestured out through the wrought iron bars that lined the balcony.

She nodded. "I never much liked big swathes of water but this is quite lovely."

"Why do you do that?"

She pushed a loose strand of hair behind her ear and Nash regretted he had not been the one to do that. Her hair had been wild since they'd left Guildham House. He rather liked it that way, pulled out of her rigid style and curling around her face. He especially liked how she looked in the sunset, the warm light touching her skin, making him itch with the need to lean in and kiss her. Russell wasn't wrong about her being unlike any woman he'd ever met. Grace was the most unusual creature he'd ever known. And he really, really liked her for that.

"It helps me understand the world."

"Writing does?"

She bit down on her lip and nodded. "It's something I've done since I was a child." She lowered the notes to her lap. "I never really understood people, but I understood writing and books. Sometimes, if I just get my thoughts out onto paper, I can link a chain of evidence and understand what is occurring around me." She glanced up at him. "I know it sounds odd."

"It makes sense to me."

"I do not suppose you have ever struggled to understand the world and the people in it."

"There are certainly people in the world I do not understand."

At least, he thought there was. For many years, he had not understood his father's behavior toward him. How could a man practically disown his son? Force him to be cut off from his family? Prevent him from doing the one thing he wished to do? But he was beginning to grasp it now. Everyone had to make difficult decisions, and if Nash wrote notes about his younger self, saw himself through Grace's eyes, would he see the evidence behind his father's decision?

Unfortunately, he was beginning to think yes. Nash had been selfish, greedy, and reckless. And potentially, his father had done the only thing he could think of.

"What are you making notes about?" he asked.

She hesitated and her gaze locked with his. "You mostly."

He leaned in and gave into the desire to shove that stubborn strand of hair back behind her ear. "What do you need to understand about me?"

Her throat bobbed. "So many things," she murmured.

"Like what?"

"Like...why do you make my tummy feel all strange? Why can I think of nothing else but you? Why—" Her voice cracked.

Nash could swear his heart must have doubled in size upon hearing her words. He slid a hand across her cheek and cupped her face. "You do the same to me."

"I try to make sense of it, but I cannot."

"Perhaps you do not always have to make sense of everything."

"But I do." She frowned. "It is what I have always done."

He leaned in. "Turn that mind off for one moment, what do you want to do?"

"Kiss you."

"Then I think you should follow your instinct and kiss me."

"But instincts are not always—"

He pressed his lips to hers, unwilling to wait a moment longer to taste her. Her eyelids fluttered closed, and she moaned. He drew in a shuddering breath through his nostrils and pressed the kiss deep and hard, slipping his tongue into her mouth and tasting her. His body responded instantly, growing harder by the second when she curled her fingers into his arms. The slight bite of fingernails combined with the fresh breeze coming in off the lake kept his senses sharp, able to feel every little thing about the kiss.

He shifted closer, moving his hands down to her rear. She shifted with him, straddling his lap and looping her arms around his neck. He groaned at the feel of her delicate body nestled just so against him. She wriggled to get comfy and stars lit behind his eyelids.

Trailing kisses away from her mouth, he nibbled her jawline, her neck, her lobe. She arched into his touches and her nipples pressed against his chest, like tiny pebbles. He used one hand to palm a breast and moved back up to her mouth. She rocked into him and kissed him furiously.

"I'm not meant to touch you," he reminded her.

Or was he reminding himself?

"It is a little too late for that."

It was far, far too late for that. He was lost to this woman, drowning in his need for her. Russell and Guy could be standing in the damned doorway and he still did not think he would be able to deny her. Grace prided herself on being rational, but he couldn't even grasp a single thread of ration whilst he had her in his arms.

GRACE HAD TRIED. So hard. But it was no good. There was no discovering the reason behind her attraction to Nash. No fathoming why their relationship did not boil down to simply two people unable to ignore their basic instinct to procreate.

It was so, so much more than that and no matter what she did to try to understand it, there was no understanding to be had.

All she knew was that she needed his touch, needed him nearby. When she woke alone, she missed him. She had known few men, but she didn't need to know many to understand there were few like Nash.

Using her hold on him as leverage, she rocked against him. Sensations sparked in her body and she leaned back and closed her eyes again. He continued to trail kisses down her neck and nibbled her earlobe, sending tiny trails of pleasure down her spine. None of this felt like a simple need to follow what human nature desired. It felt more complex and far less rational.

She could not regret it, though. Being in Nash's arms made her feel so many things. Not just pleasure but strength and boldness. The Grace who had arrived at Guildham would never have rubbed herself against a man's cock for goodness sakes.

She opened her eyes to find him watching her as she rode him. Their gazes locked and she struggled to draw breath. So much raw desire lingered behind his eyes, his pupils wide and dark. A sure sign of arousal, she knew that, but it was more than that. Under that gaze, she was sensuous and beautiful and far from being the boyish creature she had always thought she was. He watched her as though she were a drop of rain in the middle of a drought and he needed to lap her up.

Sweet Lord, she hoped he did.

They had hardly any time left together, and she wanted it all.

"Yes," he moaned as she moved harder. He palmed one breast then the other, encouraging her on with a hand to her back.

She rocked and rocked until it became too much. The pleasure splintered, a sweet little pulse that turned into a wave and washed through her. She stiffened, allowing it to overtake her, then collapsed against Nash's chest.

He rubbed a hand up and down her back, murmuring sweet words in her ear—talk of her beauty, of her passion. Nash had unlocked a woman she did not know existed and she had little idea how to return to normal.

Finally, she lifted her head.

He kissed her mouth gently. "Did that help you understand?"

She shook her head. "Not one jot."

He stilled and cocked his head. "Damn, that was Guy."

Grace froze too and heard Guy calling Nash's name. He eased her away with a grip on her arms and hastily stood. "I shouldn't have come to you," he muttered.

"Nash—"

"I had better go. Get some sleep," he ordered.

"But, Nash—"

"Sleep."

He twisted, nearly stumbling over Claude in his haste to escape. Grace stared at the door once he'd closed it then glanced at her notes. She understood a few things now at least. She was falling for him. Or perhaps she had already fallen for him. But he continued to fight it. She did not begrudge him his honor, but this was bigger than some vow and she was getting tired of him denying it.

Chapter Twenty-Four

Grace paused by the window that looked over the rear garden and lowered Claude to the ground. "Be a good boy," she ordered.

She opened the door swiftly and shut it behind her before the cat could follow. Claude had settled in once he had been offered some cold slices of meat and a comfy spot by the fire, but he would still try to escape if he could.

She did not much blame him.

Being in the same house as these three men was an odd experience. She'd never been privy to so much masculinity. They all stalked around as though danger was around the corner, despite the fact they constantly reassured her there was no danger of her being found here. Russell and Guy were what she considered brooding types. Guy, in particular, was not prone to smiling and though Russell had a more relaxed manner to him, she was never certain how to engage him.

She would be glad when it was over.

Except she wouldn't.

It seemed mightily unfair she would have to return to a normal life after this. How could she read and play cards with her aunt and adopt more stray cats when she had been through so much with him? It hardly seemed fair that life should throw all of this at her then expect her to hide away and live a humble, dull life.

She wrinkled her nose. How much had changed in such a short time. Her previous ambitions no longer filled her with anticipation.

She strode up the garden path to where Nash was standing. His shoulders were silhouetted against the afternoon sun, making her itch to spread her palms over them and press herself against his back in an attempt to absorb whatever he could offer her.

She had concluded there was no understanding why there was a pull between them, one that was certainly about more than procreation, and for once, she had stopped trying to understand. All she wanted from Nash was to *feel*. No more thinking or even overthinking. Just feeling.

But he'd left her after that kiss, that moment. A kiss that still made her toes curl. A kiss she was certain he'd felt to his very bones, just like her. Yet he had been able to leave her as though it was nothing. And then she had not seen him until now.

She needed answers.

He turned when she was nearly upon him. His jaw tensed. "Grace."

Lord, just him saying her name made her blood run hot. She wanted to hear him say it more except she wanted him to utter the word against her bare skin.

"What are you doing?"

He glanced at his feet. "Keeping watch."

"But I'm not in danger."

"No, you are not," he confirmed. "But it does not hurt to be cautious."

"I suppose not." She laced her fingers together. "I was hoping we could talk."

"You should go inside." He nodded toward the door. "It's getting cold."

"Are you avoiding me?"

"Grace, I'm keeping watch," he said, turning back to look out over the valley rising up away from the building.

She moved around to stand in front of him and folded her arms. "I'm not leaving until we talk."

"Go inside," he said tightly.

"No."

He shook his head. "Why do women have to be so stubborn?"

"Probably because we are fed up with being told what to do."

"All I'm asking is that you go inside."

"And avoid talking, of course. Such a masculine thing to do." She pursed her lips. "You know there is research to suggest a man's inclination to wish to remain silent can do quite a lot of damage to their brain function."

"Of course there is." His lips tilted. "Very well, what did you wish to speak of?"

"Yesterday evening."

He groaned. "Grace, there is nothing to say about it."

"I think there is."

"It was a very nice evening, is that what you were after?"

"It was," she agreed. "So why did you run away from me?"

"I did not run away."

"You certainly did. You nearly tripped over Claude in the process."

His jaw tensed and she saw the muscles there work.

"Why did you run away?" she pressed.

"I did not run away," he bit out. "I was simply trying to be a gentleman."

She lifted a brow. "I think it is a bit late for that."

"Don't I know it," he muttered.

"Pardon?"

"Damn it, Grace. I tried so hard to resist you but you're impossible with your big eyes and even bigger brain and your little notes and the way you say whatever is on your mind."

She blinked several times.

"I failed at being a gentleman once and I'm trying not to fail again."

"What if I do not wish you to be a gentleman?"

He gave her a sad smile. "Grace, just go inside. I do not think these circumstances are right to discuss this."

"I'll be going home before long. Will we ever get to discuss this?"

He shrugged. "Perhaps not."

Grace shook her head. "I never really understood why men make women angry, but I can see why now. We have the reputation for being the silly, stubborn sex, but it is men who are the ones who are mule-headed and foolish."

"Grace—"

"You have made it clear now, that you desire me. That you like me, I think. You would not say such things about my person and how I behave if you did not like me, yet you are willing to deny us both something we need because of some notion that society has put upon us."

"Damn it, Grace, that is not—"

She swiveled on her heel and marched back inside before he could finish his sentence. For the first time in her life, she was angry. It flowed through her, all hot and spiky.

She smiled to herself.

Oddly enough, she rather liked it.

She had spoken up for herself, for her sex, and this was about the strongest she had ever felt in her life.

FINGERS LACED BEHIND his head, Nash peered up at the bare ceiling above. There was nothing of interest apart from a cobweb that kept dancing in the draught that seeped in around the edge of the window. Unlike home, there was no cornicing or interesting wood canopies to study.

He damn well wished there was. Anything to distract him. A damned cobweb wasn't going to do the job unfortunately.

Not when he knew Grace was in the bedroom next door and she was angry with him.

He'd never seen anything like it. She was damned impressive when angry. And not really wrong. The horse had bolted, and he was trying to close the gate. Doing a terrible job of it too. Making love to her then running away and trying to dismiss her. He was making one big, awful mess of this whole thing and he had no idea how to fix that.

He could confess to all his past for one. The thought made his blood run cold. She would most certainly be angry at him for that. Then he could confess to Guy all that had occurred between them.

Easier said than done. Guy wasn't known for being the understanding, calm sort. The Kidnap Club would be over for him.

He blew out a breath. It had to happen, he supposed. Tomorrow he'd tell Guy he'd messed up and he understood if he wanted nothing more to do with him. Then he'd tell Grace that he had also messed up his past—that he really wasn't a gentle-man. That he was no better than her greedy uncle, taking all he could and throwing it away on cards and caring little for the im-pact his greed had.

Lord, how bloody awful that all sounded. Yet it was the right thing to do. Come clean about everything and take it all on the chin. No more hiding from his past and pretending he had been the one wronged and no hiding from his current mis-takes either.

Not that he could think of Grace as a mistake. Without her, he'd be walking around like a damned fool still, blaming his fa-ther for his own failings.

A floorboard outside squeaked. He froze, forcing his breaths to become shallow.

It couldn't be her. She was still angry with him.

He didn't want it to be either. Then he'd have to tell her everything sooner. And yet again try to resist her. It was too damned exhausting not being near her and taking her into his arms.

Light, padding footsteps went past his door then stopped. It couldn't be Russell or Guy. Far too delicate. It had to be her.

God, he wanted it to be.

The footsteps padded past again then light slipped under the crack of the door. He pushed himself up in bed. He didn't want her here.

But he did.

Every muscle, every fiber of him needed it to be her.

The door eased open and warm candlelight filled the room. He held his breath as Grace slipped in and eased the door shut behind her. "Are you alone?" she whispered.

He nodded, his tongue thick, his throat refusing to work. She'd come to him, despite his behavior, and he couldn't be more damned grateful.

"Were you sleeping?"

He shook his head.

She moved slowly over to his bed like some ethereal creature, her footsteps hardly making a sound. The scent of soap followed her, and he longed to reach out for her, but he was frozen. Every breath he took hurt and he knew that wouldn't cease until she was in his arms. Lowering the candle onto the table at the side of the bed, she came to stand beside the bed, her hands twined together in front of her. The warm light drew his attention to her wide eyes, her soft cheeks, her delicate mouth, and the fragileness of her frame.

Yet there was nothing fragile about her tonight. She exuded strength and confidence with her lifted chin and determined stance. He imagined she might even be able to take the truth about his past.

"We do not need to make love if you do not wish."

He offered out a hand and she slipped her fingers into his. Then he lifted back the blankets and she slid in beside him. His voice refused so work still. No charming words of apology or even confessions would escape him. She had him frozen with desire, paralyzed by his feelings for her. All he could do was slip an arm around her and draw her to him.

"I just needed to feel your touch," she confessed.

It was all sorts of wrong. He should send her away. Tell her he couldn't break his promise to Guy again. Or own up to his past and see if she still wanted him after that.

He didn't have the strength that she did to be so courageous. She made him so weak with need that all he could do was move to press her down into the bed and stare at her for a few heartbeats before bringing his mouth to hers. She moaned against his lips and he tasted her deeply, feeling the pain in his chest and muscles ease, every inch of him softening now that he had what he craved.

Nash was condemning himself and he couldn't bring himself to care.

Chapter Twenty-Five

Nash glanced at Guy's expression as he stepped into the kitchen and his blood turned cold. "What is it?" he demanded. "What's happened? Is Grace safe?" He turned on his heel.

Russell grabbed his arm and pulled him to a halt, forcing him to face both men.

Guy folded his arms and Nash tugged away from Russell's hold. "What's going on?" He recognized the steely look on Guy's face and it never meant anything good.

"I saw her last night," Guy said, after several beats of silence.

Nash stilled. "Saw what exactly?" he forced himself to ask lightly.

They exchanged a look and Guy pushed away from where he was leaning against the table. "Damn it, Nash, have you really been bedding her?"

He let his shoulders drop. He could lie. Maybe Guy even wanted him to. But of all the things he'd been, a liar wasn't one of them. He nodded slowly.

"God damn it," Guy muttered. He shoved both hands through his hair. "You were meant to protect her, not bloody ruin her."

"I do know that, Guy," Nash said tightly. He sucked in a deep breath. He didn't want this to happen, didn't mean for it to, but asking him to stay away from Grace was like asking him not to take his next painful breath.

It was impossible.

"Told you he liked her." Russell gnawed on the end of a thumb.

Guy shook his head. "I figured you cared for her, but I didn't realize you'd go this far. I should have known bringing you on board was a mistake."

Nash straightened. "It wasn't. I've always done my job and done it well. Those women wanted for nothing and I might not have felt for them like I do Grace, but I would have done whatever was necessary to keep them safe."

"It's true," Russell said. "He always did a fine job with the women—especially those who wouldn't stop weeping. Lord knows I wouldn't have known what to do with them."

"I had one rule, Nash." Guy held up a finger. "One bloody rule."

"Do you think I don't know that?" Nash bit out. "I tried my damnedest but Grace...she's different. She got under my skin, made me question everything."

"Made you question your vows?" Guy gave him a look. "When I came to you, you were the one muttering about how your father betrayed you and you needed the coin."

"I know." Nash glanced at the floor.

There were no excuses. He'd gone back on a promise, something he said he would never do. Betraying Guy's trust hurt—deeply—but he wasn't certain he could have ever done anything differently. He needed Grace and she had woken him up. He felt like a man who'd been asleep for the past five years and she had opened his eyes to the world. Her kindness, her cleverness, her odd way of looking at things had taught him so much.

"I don't know how we're going to continue from here." Guy pinched the bridge of his nose.

"It's going to be bloody hard to trust you from now on."

"To be fair to Nash, he's never slipped up before," Russell said.

Nash was grateful for Russell's support, but he wasn't certain he deserved it. He knew he was breaking his promise, but he couldn't help himself.

"I should have known," Guy muttered. "That's what happens when you trust a gambler."

Nash scowled. "Now wait a minute. I made a mistake, but I've always been loyal, and I haven't touched a card in years."

"I know." Guy sighed. "I know, damn it, and we've been through a lot together. I considered you a friend even when you were in the thick of it and I consider you one now. But what sort of man would I be if I put people's lives in your hands, knowing you might well have a fling with one of them?"

"It's not a bloody fling!" Russell and Guy stared at him. He unfurled his hands and straightened. "It's not a fling," Nash repeated. "I love her."

Russell lifted his brows. "You love her?"

He nodded.

"In truth?" Guy asked.

He nodded again. "Believe me, Guy, if I wanted to just bed someone, you think I'd be so foolish to do it in front of you? And let's face it, she's making a fool out of me for certain, and I can't help but go along for the ride. I love her."

He'd known it for a while perhaps. It had been eating away inside of him, killing him in this sweet, silent way. To say the words aloud and admit the truth felt like he'd lifted a mountain off his shoulders.

Russell's lips quirked. "Never thought you had the ability to fall in love, Nash, but didn't I say, Guy?" He turned to Guy. "I said there was something different about her."

Guy leaned back against the kitchen table. "You love her?"

"Yes."

He lifted his hands. "I suppose...this makes things different."

"Even if they didn't, I could not help how I feel," Nash said firmly.

"What are you going to do about it?" Russell said.

Nash shrugged. "I'm still trying to figure that bit out."

Russell folded his arms. "Does she love you?"

"It's hard to say. Grace usually says what she is thinking so..."

"She hasn't said she loves you?" Russell leaned in. "That's not good."

"Besides which I haven't told her about my past properly yet."

Guy rubbed his jaw. "Most men have a past."

"Not one riddled with debt and gambling and recklessness."

Russell snorted. "That sounds like half the gentry."

"It goes against everything she believes in," Nash explained, "and I've been too cowardly to tell her I've been lying to her the whole time."

"Well, I think you might have your chance." Russell glanced behind him.

GRACE SWUNG HER gaze between all three men. She really needed to cease listening in on their conversations. They all shuffled their feet and stared at the ground or the ceiling or anywhere apart from her.

But if she had not come into the room, she would not have heard what Nash had said. She tilted her head. "You have been lying to me?"

His Adam's apple bobbed, and he glanced at the other men then stepped forward and took her arm. "Let us talk."

She nodded, taking a deep, stifled breath. There was no sense in jumping to conclusions until she had all the facts laid out in front of her. It didn't make her stomach tighten any less, however.

Nash led her into the parlor room, where a hearty fire roared, keeping the damp, dull day at bay. He shut the door behind them and strode over to the fire, giving it an aggressive prod with the poker before setting it back on its hook. Finally, he looked at her.

"I wanted to tell you many times." He frowned and straightened. "It didn't seem any great thing at first but as time went on, I realized I had been keeping it from you deliberately."

"Keeping what from me?" She scowled and took a few paces forward. "Is this about my uncle? Or Worthington? Or about who betrayed us?" She closed her mouth and motioned for him to continue.

"You are safe," he reminded her. "But there are some things you should know about me."

"About you?"

He nodded gravely and her stomach tightened further. She'd known he was holding back, of course she did. He hated talking of his family and it had only been through her observations and persistence that she knew what she did but, for some reason, not having the full information had ceased bothering her. How foolish. One should never draw a conclusion on half the information. She knew that well.

He motioned for her to sit and she did so while he rested his elbow on the mantelpiece and rubbed his forehead with his thumb and forefinger.

"By your posture, I would say it is some grim thing and you would be better off telling it to me simply and without hesitation."

He gave a dry chuckle. "I will try my best, but, Grace, it is not so easy to be rational and logical around you sometimes. This is no excuse but only a reason as to why I did not tell you all of this before."

She waited, hands folded in her lap.

He straightened and clasped his hands behind his back. "I am the heir to a viscountcy."

She nodded.

"After Cambridge, I had little with which to keep me occupied." He held up a hand. "Again, no excuse, I realize that now."

She nodded again.

"I lived a typical rakish lifestyle for a while but found it full and boring. Eventually, I started frequenting the gaming hells. There I found I had a knack for cards."

"Gaming seems to be a typical sort of an occupation for a nobleman."

"It is. But I took it to the extreme."

"Extreme?"

He sighed. "I ended up in a lot of debt. Ridiculous amounts of it. I couldn't stop gambling and my father was forced to sell off land to cover my debts. Unfortunately, that did not stop me, and I accrued more debt. Even my way of living ensured that the amount owed continued to mount. I ate the best, dressed the best, lived the best, all the while gambling away more."

"Like my uncle," she said softly. Grace swallowed hard and observed his harrowed expression.

"Indeed." He blew out a heavy breath. "There is more unfortunately. When it was clear I would not change my ways, my father cut me off. Thanks to my ego, this meant me never seeing the rest of my family again." He turned and stared into the fire, his fingers blanching where he grasped them so tightly behind his back. "I hated him for it. I thought he had taken my sisters and mother from me and worst of all, broken a promise."

"What promise was that?"

"I was to have the funds to fix Guildham House. I was to make it my home once it was done." He smiled sadly. "It was one of my ambitions as a young man. I'd always loved staying there as a child and...I don't know...it represented a sort of independence I suppose. So when my father cut me off, I decided to make my home there—as if to make some sort of stubborn point. Of course, I had nowhere else to go either."

"I see."

"It was a fine job Guy came along really. He offered me work and I've been able to support myself and slowly repair the house. It will take a lot more than I have, naturally, but it's enough to ensure it doesn't completely crumble."

"And your father made no attempt to contact you?"

"Even if he did, I would not have accepted it." He turned to face her. "My pride was wounded, and I am a shallow man it seems."

"Why did you not tell me this?"

"I thought it irrelevant to begin with. Then I realized you might well hate me for being like your uncle." He grimaced. "I couldn't bear the thought of you hating me." He stepped over to her and dropped to his knees in front of her. "You might well hate me now and I would not blame you."

She eyed him, taking in his pained expression. She shook her head slowly. "As if I could hate you," she whispered.

"Then you forgive me?"

"I understand why you kept quiet about it." She pursed her lips. "I am not certain of anything else."

His shoulders dropped. "I understand."

"I need some time to think on the situation."

He nodded dejectedly. "Of course you do." Nash strode out of the room suddenly, barely giving her a moment to utter his name.

She blew out a breath. He had hidden things from her—deliberately. But did that change how she felt about him?

Chapter Twenty-Six

"We'll find him, I promise," Russell muttered as Nash entered the kitchen.

He looked between Russell and Grace, his gut tightening. "Find who?"

Russell glanced at the floor and kicked aside a dry leaf from the stone floor. "The damned cat."

"Claude?" Nash turned his attention to Grace. He'd not spoken to her properly since yesterday and he had no idea if she had forgiven him yet. She needed time to think but about what? About him being a liar? Or a gambler? Or a stubborn ass who should have made his peace with his father long ago?

Part of him feared if she thought too hard, she'd realize she was too damned good for him.

Grace nodded, lifting her chin. Arms folded, she faced down the long-limbed Russell, and if it wasn't for how Nash felt at present, he would find it quite amusing that such a small woman was capable of making the man's shoulders drop. Russell looked guilty as hell.

"What happened?"

"Russell left the window open and Claude escaped," she explained.

"Only for a moment," Russell protested.

"One moment too long." She shook her head. "He is out there all alone now, probably scared and lost."

Russell made a face. "He's been gone for no more than a minute." He pressed fingers to either side of his head. "I tried to grab him as he went but the blighter scratched me." He revealed claw marks on his arm to Nash.

"Looks like you got what you deserve," Nash said with a slight smile.

"Well, thank you for your sympathy," he muttered.

"You did let the cat loose. It was the one thing Grace asked you not to do."

"You are hardly a paragon." Russell glared at him. "Haven't you broken a promise a time or two?"

Nash groaned inwardly. Russell knew how to strike him deep. He turned his attention to Grace. "Any idea where he might have gone?"

"Oh yes, he told me he might take a little wander around the lake..."

He blinked at Grace.

"Of course, I do not know. He's a cat, Nash." Her eyes shimmered and Nash took a step forward and curled his fingers around her arms, forcing her to look at him.

"We'll find him," he vowed.

"I hope so." She bit down on her bottom lip. "He might have been wild once but he's...he's too pampered now. He needs me."

Claude wasn't the only one. Nash sympathized with the cat. One night apart from her and he already missed her.

"Let us make haste and hunt him down. He can't have gone far."

She gave him a look. "Cats are fast, you know."

"I don't think I've ever seen Claude do anything fast. I'm certain we shall find him straight away," he assured her, despite having little idea if they'd ever find the cat again. He prayed they did, though. He wouldn't want to see Grace upset for the world and he'd already done enough of that. Losing her cat on top of everything else would be horrible for her. And, well, he had to admit, he had a little bit of admiration for Claude himself. When he curled up on a chair, he was rather pettable and Claude had taken to nuzzling Nash's hand when he wanted a fuss. It was quite sweet really.

He groaned inwardly. What the devil had happened to him? Thinking cats were sweet and fearing the opinion of a woman?

Not just any woman, though. Grace. The woman had tied him up in some strange knot and he wasn't certain he'd ever free himself from it.

He wasn't certain he *wanted* to be free from it.

"Come, let us find him." He pointed to Russell. "Why don't you start searching the grounds?"

Russell rolled his eyes. "I can't pick him up if I find him. The cat hates me."

"Cats are very sensitive," Grace said. "If he hates you, there's a reason for it."

"I haven't done anything wrong," he mumbled. He walked past Nash and murmured to him, "She looks sweet, but she has a vicious tongue when she wants to."

Nash chuckled. He couldn't help be proud of Grace for giving Russell a scolding. God knew, every man needed a scolding occasionally and it was quite a sight to see her standing up to the giant that was Russell.

He slipped on his coat and waited for Grace to put on hers then they headed outside. "At least it's not raining," he said. "Claude will stay warm and dry."

"Wherever he is." She peered around the front garden, ducking down to look under a bush before straightening. "Nash, what if we do not find him?"

"We shall." He offered out a hand and his heart did a foolish dance when she took it. It didn't mean anything. Didn't mean she had forgiven him, he told himself. She simply needed comfort at present.

They moved briskly through the front garden, pausing every now and then to check out some shadowy spot where the cat could be hiding, but with no luck. He pushed open the gate and they followed a path worn in the grass that wound its way down to the lake. The rain had decided to let up today and there were even a few spots of blue in the sky, releasing the occasional flickers of bright, warm sunlight. It would at least make it easier to hunt for Claude, though he had little idea how far a cat could go in minutes or where they were inclined to go.

"Should we be searching anywhere in particular?"

"It's hard to say. Cats are curious creatures. He could be anywhere."

He squeezed her fingers and they continued down the path. The lake glittered in the sunlight, spread wide across the valley. On the opposite side, trees lined the edge of the water and a small island sat in the center of it, dotted with some bare-looking trees. He rather regretted they were not taking this walk for nice reasons.

He also rather regretted he couldn't stop and take her in his arms and kiss her until they were both breathless. He caught her glaring at him and turned his attention back to looking for the cat. It seemed she had certainly not forgiven him yet.

GRACE SCOWLED. NASH did not seem to be concentrating on looking for Claude at all. He kept getting some odd, faraway look in his eyes as though he were imagining being somewhere else. She might have put it down to not wishing to be with her a few weeks ago but after his confession yesterday, she wasn't convinced of that. He had spoken to her in a way no one ever had, and she could not deny it had touched her.

But that touched her heart. Not her head. She needed to think seriously about this. About him. Weigh everything up and come to a conclusion.

The trouble was, she suspected she had already come to one—she just didn't know what to do with it. So many years spent under the control of a man and she was so near her freedom. How could she give that chance up?

A sound caught her attention and she tugged Nash to a standstill and pressed a finger to her lips. She scanned the grass around them but there was no sign of a black, furry thing skulking about. "Did you hear that?"

He shook his head.

"There." It was definitely a meow—a rather plaintive one at that. "That has to be Claude."

"I heard it then." He released her hand and moved in the direction of the sound.

She followed, pausing between meows to listen intently. "He sounds distressed."

"At least it seems to be coming from one place." Nash pointed to a mound of grass. "From there, I think."

Grace hastened over. "Claude? Here, kitty, kitty, kitty," she cooed.

Claude meowed in response, a long, drawn out sound that made her bottom lip quiver.

"Claude, where are you?"

Nash clambered up the slight mound and grimaced. "In here by the looks of it."

"Oh no." Using her hands, she scrabbled her way up to join Nash. Not far from where he was standing was a burrow dug into the dirt. She just made out the glint of Claude's eyes in the darkness. Getting down onto her knees, she put her hand into the hole. "Come here, Claude. Mama is here."

She pushed her hand all the way down to her shoulder but felt nothing, no brush of fur or even a swipe of claws. Withdrawing her arm, she looked up at Nash. "He's either stuck or too scared to move."

He tugged off his jacket, undid his cufflinks, and shoved them in his pockets, then rolled up his shirt sleeves. "I have longer arms than you."

She tried to force her attention away from his arms, where sinew and veins threaded along his sunkissed skin. Now was most certainly not the time to be thinking about his arms—or the things he could be doing to her with them. Like holding her, caressing her, touching her...

No. She was here for Claude, not to obsess over Nash's arms.

He got to his knees and shoved his arm all the way in. "Still can't reach him," he grunted. He moved back and used his hands to dig away some of the dirt. Grace dropped down to help him, using her fingers to help.

"Let me try again." He pressed his arm in the hole again and Claude made a sound of protest which Grace could only assume meant Nash had him. "He's stuck I think."

They dug some more until they could see that Claude had wedged himself tight into the hole. Nash shook his head. "Claude, I thought you were a good boy."

"He is normally."

"I know," he said. "We'll get him out."

He dug some more, creating enough space for both arms to fit down the hole. She chewed on her bottom lip while he pushed his arms deeper. Slowly, he withdrew muddy arms and tugged out Claude with a flourish. The cat, filthy and more mussed up than normal, looked askew at Nash, as though he had been quite content to stay in his hole, thank you very much.

"Here we go," Nash announced. "One filthy, annoyed cat."

"Oh, thank you!" Grace took the offered cat, holding him tight against her in one arm before flinging her arm around Nash's waist and stretching onto tiptoes to give him a kiss on the cheek. "Thank you, thank you, thank you."

He shrugged. "Anything for you, Grace."

Taking a step back, she eyed him. His expression was sincere, and she did not doubt his words one jot. Whatever had been in his past, he was not that man any longer. She doubted the Nash of old would rescue cats or offer up any piece of his soul to someone like her. And yet he had.

She blew out a breath and held the wriggling cat to her chest. His past did not matter, but her future did. She loved him and no notes or studies of him would persuade her different-ly. The knowledge beat hard in her heart, rippling through her veins and whispering in her mind.

She loved him.

But what was she going to do about it?

Chapter Twenty-Seven

Nash stumbled out of bed before he quite understood why, his heart was smashing against his rib cage. He nearly tripped over the blankets as they tangled around his legs and he fumbled with them, cursing over and over. "Damn it, bugger, bloody thing." He finally unwound the sheet and flung open the door to find Russell standing in the hallway, a candle holder clutched in one hand.

"What is it?"

Russell gave him a grim look. "The uncle is here."

Nash's heart decided hammering like a bloody hammer wasn't good enough anymore and came to a sharp, sudden stop. "Grace's uncle?"

"Indeed."

"How the bloody hell did he find us?"

Russell lifted both shoulders. "Lord knows."

Nash glanced at Grace's firmly shut bedroom door. "He cannot have her." He frowned and looked Russell up and down. "Where's Guy and why the devil haven't you beaten the snot out of her uncle?"

"The man came peacefully. Alone." Russell shrugged again.

"What the devil..." Nash murmured.

"Put some clothes on. You'd be better off speaking to him. You know Grace the best."

He threaded his fingers through his hair. "I'll be hard pushed to simply talk to the cad. He tried to sell off his niece."

Russell put a hand to Nash's shoulders. "If this can be solved peacefully, we should ensure it. He has seen us now. It could put everything in jeopardy."

Nash cursed under his breath. "It's a strange day when *you* should be talking of peace."

"I only use violence when absolutely necessary."

Nash eyed him. "Like that time when you punched the chap who wouldn't cease singing ballads in the Royal Oak?"

"That was entirely necessary." Russell's expression didn't change.

Blowing out a breath, Nash went back into the bedroom and threw on enough clothes to look vaguely respectable. Not that he cared what the uncle thought. The man could go hang as far as he was concerned, and if he was alone, there was no chance he was even setting eyes on Grace.

He stepped out of the bedroom and his heart gave another jolt. He glowered at Grace. "Good Lord, woman, someone is determined to give me a heart attack tonight."

She peered at him through a veil of mussed hair. "What is going on? I heard Russell talking of my uncle."

He could lie but she would only find out or draw her own conclusions easily enough. Trust him to fall for a woman with a giant mind. "He is here."

Her eyes widened and she blew the hair unsuccessfully from her face. With a sound of annoyance, she shoved it aside and tucked it behind her ear. "Here? In this cottage?"

"Yes. We found him skulking around outside."

"But how did he find us?"

"I do not know but I intend to find out." He put a hand to her arm. "Go back in your room and lock the door. We shall have him sent on his way soon enough."

She pursed her lips then finally shook her head. "No, I do not think so."

"Pardon?"

She tightened the string at the neck of her shift and reached behind the door, drawing out a robe. Stuffing her arms into the sleeves, she tightened that too until he could see the fragile outline of her waist. She reminded him rather of a knight suiting up for battle. Her shoulders rose and she lifted her chin. "I think I should speak with him."

"Grace, you really do not have to—"

"I do."

"Grace—"

"I do, Nash. Being with you, doing all of this," she gestured vaguely around the hallway, "it has at least taught me I am more capable than I thought. I will speak with him."

"I'm really not comfortable—"

"Nash," she said firmly, "I have had men tell me what to do my whole life. I am certainly not going to listen to you now." She patted his shoulder. "Besides, if I do not talk to him, what will happen? He shall only reveal the three of you. It seems most logical that I try to reason with him."

He opened his mouth then closed it. Hell, he couldn't help admire her. This man had dictated what had to be a miserable existence and she could easily tell him to go thrash the man then send him on his way. He only hoped her idea of reasoning with him was not to give in to her uncle's demands.

He led the way downstairs and found the three men in the kitchen. Russell stood by the door, blocking the exit whilst Guy remained standing by the sink, leaned back against the porcelain, his arms folded.

However, nothing was nonchalant about his posture for which Nash was grateful. The uncle sat at the table, peering up at both men, his eyes wide. Rounded in figure with thinning hair and dressed in fine clothing, Nash saw nothing threatening in the man.

That did not mean, however, Nash intended to relax.

"What do you want?" he demanded.

Grace put a hand to his arm and moved past him. She remained standing at Nash's side and he caught the tiniest tremor moving through her body. As much as he wished he could tuck her behind him or put a comforting arm around her shoulders, he managed to keep his arms firmly folded across his chest. Grace had asked to speak with him, and he'd let that happen, but if the man said anything disrespectful...Hell's teeth, he was not sure he could be held responsible for his actions.

THE TENSION IN the room made Grace shiver. She spied Nash's blanched knuckles out of the corner of her eye. He was like a horse, waiting to bolt, so she needed to ensure the situation remained calm. However her uncle found them, he knew now who was involved and he could cause a great deal of grief for the three men who tried to help her. There was no chance she was letting anything happen to them, especially when they would go on to help other women in her situation in the future.

And she could never let Nash come to harm.

"Grace." Uncle Charlie smiled. "You are unscathed. How wonderful." He looked between the men. "I do not know what is happening here, but I am taking my niece away." He waved a finger at Russell. "I warn you, if you try to harm me..."

Russell took a step forward, his lips a thin line, his eyes cold. Her uncle shrank down into the chair.

"They will not harm you, Uncle," she said, shooting a warning look at Russell. He huffed and took a step back. "But you will not be taking me away either. Did Aunt Elsie tell you where I was?"

He scowled. "No. Why the devil would she know where you were? You wish to stay with your kidnappers?" He went to rise from the chair then thought twice about it and sank down. "Good Lord, I have heard of this before. Women seduced by their kidnappers, their minds warped by them. I always knew you were a silly girl, but I never expected—"

Nash slammed a fist down on the table. "She is no silly girl," he said through gritted teeth.

Grace motioned for him to stand back and drew out a chair to sit opposite her uncle. She eyed him dispassionately. How odd it was that he scared her so not that long ago. Now she only saw a sad little man, trying to make up for his lack of, well, anything, by spending money on clothes and belongings. He wasn't like Nash, who could have done the same with his earnings, but instead put it into reviving the house he loved so much.

"I will return home," she said.

"Like hell," Nash hissed.

"When I am ready," she continued. "After my birthday."

Her uncle shook his head wildly. "We have the marriage license. You must marry Worthington. I promised you to him."

"I was not yours to promise."

"I am still your guardian," her uncle snapped. "I can damn well do what I like with you."

"Not anymore, Uncle Charlie." She laced her fingers together. "I will be one-and-twenty in two days, and you cannot decide my fate."

Her uncle's cheeks reddened. "I can and I will. I'll have you dragged away from here. No court in the land will let this stand. And all of you will hang for this."

A scoff escaped Guy. "You think you can make it out of here alive to tell your tale?"

"I...I..." Uncle Charlie's face looked as though it might explode. He shifted in his seat.

"Uncle, I have no wish to see you harmed," she said softly. "But you cannot tell anyone of what these men have done."

He scowled. "Why on earth not? They must have terrified you, must have hurt you in some way. They are kidnappers, Grace!"

"They have done a lot to help me," she explained slowly, "and I will not have you cause them any harm."

"Then come home with me and perhaps I shall forget it all."

"Uncle—"

"She cannot come home with you," Nash interrupted. "Because we are engaged to be married."

Grace twisted in her seat to eye Nash, her mouth ajar. That was certainly unexpected.

"Engaged?" Uncle Charlie's eyes bulged. "To your kidnapper?"

"We plan to marry shortly, do we not, darling?" Nash said, resting a hand on her shoulder. "I'm a viscount which I think should please you greatly, and if you say anything about what we do, you shall have a criminal in the family. Are you certain you wish that?"

Her uncle looked between her and Nash. "Is this true?"

It would be so easy—a logical, ideal solution really. But she was not certain she wanted logic. And she certainly did not want Nash to marry her out of some desperate way to save them both. There had to be a way to ensure her uncle's silence that was better than this.

She loved Nash and she would not cheapen her love like this. Nor would she let these men dictate her future to her.

"It is not true," she admitted.

Nash's hand dropped from her shoulder. "Grace—"

She couldn't bring herself to look at him. As wonderful as the idea of marriage to him was, she needed more than him swooping in to be her rescuer, more than him offering simply to save her from one man so she could be passed on to another.

"It is not true," she repeated, glancing around the room. Russell offered her the slightest of encouraging smiles and Guy remained in the same position, one eyebrow lifted. "But you will not be telling anyone what has occurred here."

"B-but—" Her uncle spluttered.

She held up a finger. "I will return home on my birthday. Once I am there, I will have my inheritance and I will offer you this—four hundred pounds for your silence."

Uncle Charlie opened his mouth then closed it several times like a fish gasping for air. Finally, his shoulders slumped. "I suppose that would be acceptable."

"Excellent." She pushed the chair back and rose from the table. "Russell, will you see my uncle out?"

He grinned. "Gladly."

Her uncle shook his head. "I do not understand what has happened here, but it is strange indeed."

"It is a little strange," she agreed, "and I am glad for it."

Chapter Twenty-Eight

Nash had thought the most painful thing to ever happen to him had been his father breaking his promise to fund the repairs to Guildham House.

Not anymore. That was a mere pinprick compared to Grace turning him down flat.

Not that he had asked for her hand in marriage in the traditional sense, but he thought he'd made it fairly clear what he was offering. And he had thought she felt the same way as he did.

Damn. How wrong could a man get?

Russell unfolded his arms and scooped a hand under the uncle's arm. Guy came to the other side of them. "Time to go," he said.

They escorted the flustered-looking man out into the dark. He only hoped they could find out how exactly the man had tracked them down. There had to be someone, somewhere who had given them up, but who it was, he could not fathom. Almost no one knew of the lake house.

He turned to Grace, but he couldn't think what to say. He shuffled his feet and eyed the floor. He wanted answers really. Why did she not love him? Was it his past? Was it something else?

"Nash, I must thank you for what you did but you must know I could not go along with the lie."

"I was quite happy to," he muttered.

"You are no liar and I would not wish you to be one."

"I am sort of." He glanced up. "That is probably why you did not wish to go along with it, I suppose."

She shook her head. "No, that is not it at all."

"Then why?"

"Because...I feel a lot of things for you."

He scowled. "For a woman who prides herself on logic, that makes no sense."

"I feel a lot of things for you, but this has been a strange time and I feel a lot of things for me too."

"Now I'm really lost."

"This time with you has taught me a lot about myself and has shown me I can be brave." She reached out to him, but he shifted out of her way. He was behaving like an ass, but he was not certain he could bear her touch right now.

"I cannot let someone tell me what to do. Not right now."

"You know damn well, I wouldn't—"

The kitchen door burst open and the uncle stumbled through. He bent double, gasping for breath.

"Uncle Charlie? What has happened?"

He remained bent over, drawing in ragged breaths. "Worthington, and his men." He straightened and gulped down some air. "They are here. Several of them. He told me where you were, but I did not think he was going to come. He told me to bring you home." He nodded toward Nash. "Your friends told me to come back here and seek shelter while they took them on. God knows the man will beat me to within an inch of my life if he finds out I agreed not to give him Grace."

"Bloody hell." Nash turned to Grace. "Take your uncle and go upstairs."

"What about you?"

"I'll have to help Guy and Russell."

"But—"

"Just do it," he barked.

Grace nodded and took her uncle's arm. "This way."

He waited until they were upstairs, and he heard the bedroom door shut before shoving his feet into his boots. The men outside were likely those ones they ran into at the inn. A dangerous lot. Guy and Russell were fighters but if the men were armed, they'd be in danger. He couldn't very well leave them to it.

If only he'd brought his bloody weapon downstairs, though.

Before he could step out of the kitchen, the back door slammed open. Nash rushed at the first man to enter, slamming him in the gut and shoving him back into the next man. He ducked a fist from God knows where and responded with a punch of his own, sending the second chap sprawling. A third pushed past them. Nash curled his lip.

"Worthington."

The older man peered down his nose at him. "Who the devil are you?"

"It doesn't much matter."

Worthington lifted his pistol as the other two men staggered to their feet. "No, I suppose it does not. Now, where is my fiancé?"

"She's most certainly not your fiancé."

"Tell me where she is," Worthington demanded.

Nash glanced around Worthington. One of the men clutched a bleeding nose and the other had a hand wrapped around his stomach. None of them had weapons in their hands so he only had Worthington's pistol to contend with. He would have to rely on the fact pistols were not very accurate unless Guy and Russell could get here quickly. He had to assume they were dealing with the rest of Worthington's men and he only hoped they were not in the same sort of trouble.

"Tell you what," Nash said. "We can fight like men. If you best me, you can have Grace."

"Grace, is it?" Worthington narrowed his gaze. "Don't tell me the silly little whore has ingratiated herself toward you."

Nash clenched his jaw. God, he hoped the man wanted a fight. He'd love to smash that smug face in and make him pay for scaring Grace. "A fight, damn it."

Worthington's lips quirked. "An honorable kidnapper. How odd. Though, I did think there was something strange when that boy told us about you."

Nash grimaced inwardly. The only boy they had helping them was Tommy Jenkins, the delivery boy. He must have told Worthington about them, though how he knew about the lake house, he didn't know. "You better not have hurt him."

"Only a little." Worthington flashed a smile. "But now I am going to hurt you."

"Not if I hurt you first."

Worthington lifted his pistol and Nash drew in a breath. If only he knew Grace would be safe, he could make his peace with dying but as it was, he could not.

The man pulled the trigger.

"HE'S GOING TO kill us both!"

Grace didn't have time to deal with her uncle's whimpering. That had been a gunshot, surely? And Nash did not have his Flintlock. She knew that because it was in her hand. She fumbled with the powder, and pushed it all down with the ramrod

Uncle Charlie's face was slick with sweat as he cowered behind the bed. "H-how do you know how to do that?"

She shook her head. To think she had been scared of this man for all those years. He was nothing but a coward.

She could not be, though. Not today. Nash needed her and she hoped to God that gunshot hadn't been for him.

If he was dead.

She shook her head. Now was not the time to think about that.

"Stay here," she ordered her uncle, ignoring his protests as she stepped out of the bedroom. How could that man offer her up to Worthington when he knew full well her fiancé was a violent man? Why would he do that to her? But those questions were for another time, a time when Nash's life wasn't in danger.

A beat pulsed hard in her fingers where she gripped the pistol and she gulped down deep breaths as she hastened downstairs. Nash might scold her for not being quiet, but his life was in danger and there was no time. She stepped out into the kitchen, brandishing the pistol.

The air left her lungs when she spied Nash prone on the floor. Bile rose in her throat and everything felt hot, like someone had lit her shift on fire and she was flaming from head to toe. Nash groaned from his position on the floor and she spotted blood seeping through his breeches, just above his knee.

Worthington fumbled with his pistol, readying himself to reload whilst three unarmed men lingered by the back door.

She lifted the pistol and pointed it at Worthington. "I would drop your weapon if I were you."

Worthington's startled gaze flew to hers. "Well, if it isn't my fiancé."

"I am not your fiancé."

"Grace," groaned Nash, using a chair to haul himself to his feet. "Go back upstairs."

She shook her head. "I suggest you leave," she told Worthington, "or I shall be forced to shoot you."

He smirked. "A little mouse like you? You would never shoot me." He offered out a hand. "Come home with me and I'll make you my wife, and we can forget all about this."

She pulled back the hammer with two fingers. "I will never be your wife."

His expression shifted and her blood turned to ice. This was the man she knew was under that sleek charm. The man his late wife had probably seen too many times. "You do not have any choice," he bit out.

"I will never be your wife," she repeated, stepping in front of Nash.

He gestured to Nash. "Is this because of him? Because of these kidnappers?"

"No." She lifted her chin. "This is because of me. I am tired of being told what to do, of living a life dictated by men."

He made a dismissive sound. "You are addled. I shall marry you then have you sent to an asylum. That will teach you to obey your fiancé." Worthington tore a powder packet with his teeth.

Grace lifted her weapon higher. The pounding in her chest had gone, the bitterness in her throat had vanished. For the first time in forever, everything was clear and calm. She did not need to analyze the situation or write notes. She knew exactly what she had to do.

"If you try to shoot either of us, I will shoot you first." She put her finger to the trigger.

"You wouldn't dare." He poured the powder into the pan then down the barrel.

"My father taught me to shoot when I was a girl," she said calmly. "It has been a while, but I think I could still aim true."

"Grace," Nash said, trying to force her behind him.

She ignored him. Nash had done so much for her. She certainly wasn't letting him get hurt again.

Worthington eyed her for a few moments then a grin slid across his lips. "You are too soft and scared, Grace. You could never hurt me, not even to save your friend here." He lifted his pistol.

"I am not scared anymore." She pulled the trigger, the recoil sending her tumbling back into Nash. A scream echoed about the room and Worthington collapsed to the floor. Grace scrambled over and snatched up Worthington's weapon then brandished it at the men. "Go or I'll shoot you too."

They wasted no time in stumbling out of the door. Once they were gone, she glanced at Worthington as he rolled around on the floor clutching his leg. "Well, I was aiming for your arm, but your leg seems fair, seeing as you did the same to Nash."

Nash stared at her, mouth wide.

She handed him the gun and pulled out a chair for him. "I had better bandage you two up, I suppose."

He nodded and sank onto the seat. The kitchen door burst open and he lifted the gun as Grace whirled around.

Guy came to a halt in front of Worthington, who still moaned and gripped his injured leg. "What the devil happened?"

"*She* happened," Nash said.

Guy looked her over as Russell barreled into the kitchen. "What happened?" Russell asked, breathlessly.

"She happened," Guy repeated.

"Well, I'll be damned," Russell muttered.

Grace smiled. *Well, I'll be damned.* That sounded about right.

Chapter Twenty-Nine

"You know, I was rather surprised you did not sweep Miss Beaumont off her feet." Guy leaned back in the chair, propping his boots up on the table.

"For a nobleman, you have no manners." Russell pushed Guy's feet from the table, pulled out a chair from the other side of the table, and sat opposite.

Nash took a swig of ale, shaking his head. "I damn well tried."

"I could have sworn she was in love with you," Russell mused. "Perhaps she woke up to what an arrogant cad you are." A slight smile curved Russell's lips, taking the sting from the insult but Nash couldn't help think it might be true. If she'd have been in love with him, she would have gone along with a pretend engagement, surely?

"She said she wanted to be in charge of her own future," Nash muttered.

Whatever the hell that meant. He shouldn't be mad, but he couldn't help feeling a little peeved. Two weeks had passed since Grace returned home and there had been no word of how she was doing or any inkling that she might just miss him.

He certainly missed her.

"Maybe she'll come around," Guy suggested. "It was rather a stressful time for her, what with her uncle and fiancé showing up at the house."

"Stressful is an understatement." Russell gestured for more drink from the serving girl.

Nash shook his head and motioned for two drinks only. "I'll be travelling most of the day. And I doubt Grace has changed her mind. Once set on a conclusion, she's not likely to change it. Besides, if she wanted me, she could have said before she left."

"She was an interesting woman, that one," Russell said. "I wouldn't be leaving her alone for too long. She's a lot wealthier now. The men will be lining up outside her door."

Nash tried not to think about that. Besides, she had been very firm on the whole thing. She needed time alone, time to be her own woman for once.

He understood, sort of, but he wished the time alone hadn't included being away from him. Grace had made it clear—she did not want to marry anyone, including him.

"So if you make up with your father, will you be retiring from our club?" Guy asked.

Nash shrugged. "I hardly expect him to reinstate my allowance and who knows if he will even open his door to me. Besides, I broke the cardinal rule. I had rather thought you would be looking for someone else to take my role."

Guy eyed him. "You *are* in love with her."

"So?"

"You never touched a woman before Grace, and I suspect now you will never touch another again."

Russell chuckled. "The man is certainly lovesick."

He wasn't wrong. The thought of even having to be charming to another woman stung. Now he understood why Guy was so bitter after his heartbreak. He shuddered. As painful as it was being without Grace, he didn't want to become the grumpy old bastard that Guy was. Somehow, he'd have to figure out a way to get over her.

He grimaced. Easier said than done. Everywhere he turned he thought of her. Heck, he'd even caught himself petting a damned cat the other day thanks to her.

"Are you sure we should continue with the club?" Nash asked. "The lake house is compromised, as is mine."

"We can find new places, and Worthington won't say a word unless he wants to go down for shooting a lord," Guy said. "And we know the uncle is too scared to reveal us."

"That he is," Russell agreed. "The man nearly pissed himself when he saw Worthington's injury."

"I hope it didn't heal as well as mine did." Nash tapped his leg. "Thankfully, it was just a graze or else I'd be going nowhere for many, many weeks."

"Worthington deserved far worse," Russell muttered.

"I'll toast to that." Nash lifted his glass and drained it.

"So once you are back from your father's, you will continue with us?" Guy pressed.

"I don't see why not." He needed something to keep his mind off the conundrum that was Grace anyway. "Mary will want to continue to help. We'll have to find some way of including her."

Guy nodded. "I think we could install her as a permanent housekeeper somewhere."

"She certainly wouldn't miss the farm."

"And what will happen to Tommy?" Russell asked. "The poor kid was terrified by Worthington."

Guy's jaw tightened. "I'm surprised you're so forgiving, considering he nearly got us all killed."

"People make mistakes, Guy," Nash said. "Lord knows, I've made a ton of them. He got a little greedy, but I think he learned his lesson."

"The fool kid thought he could get some coin without giving us away, but Worthington beat the rest of the information out of him." Guy sighed. "I guess he probably paid for his greed."

"The boy is too smart, figuring out you had the lake house rented under a different name. He must have read some of our previous letters." Guy sighed. "I must admit, I want to do something with those smarts."

"Well, I'll be back soon," Nash announced, pushing back the chair and retrieving his jacket form the back of it. "Even sooner if my father doesn't even let me through the gate."

"You're not riding, are you?" Guy glanced at his slight limp.

"I'm a fool but I'm not that damned foolish." He shoved his arms into the jacket. "I have a carriage to take me to Herefordshire."

"Anyone would think you cared about his welfare, Guy," Russell teased.

"I only care that he remains in one piece, so he continues to work his magic on the women we help," Guy grumbled.

"I will return," he vowed.

But first he had some amends to make.

THIS MIGHT HAVE been one huge mistake. Nash's stomach turned when he climbed out of the carriage and looked up at the family home. The Palladian style house had hardly changed with the exception of a few new curtains in the drawing room windows. He only hoped one thing had changed—that his father would at least accept an audience with him. He swallowed hard as the front door eased open. Definitely a mistake. Why was he willing to put himself through a humiliating confrontation with his father again?

Oh yes, because of Grace. Damn it. Her forgiving ways, her strength had taught him at least one thing—and that was to cease being a stubborn coward. If his father still did not want to see him then at least he had tried.

"Nash!" A blur of pale muslin with ribbons streaming out at all angles dashed toward him. Henrietta flung her arms around his waist and he staggered back from the unexpected weight of her.

"Good God, you have grown." He looked down at his youngest sister who offered a gappy smile in return. His heart gave a pang. He'd missed so much, especially in Henrietta's life. And it had all been his damned fault, he knew that now. As much as he'd like to blame his father, it was his own stubbornness and stupidity that had kept him away. "When the devil did you get so big?"

"I'm tall for my age." Henrietta stepped back, clasped her hands behind her, and rocked on her heels. "Mr. Joules says you are here to speak with Papa." She bit down on her bottom lip. "You won't argue like last time and go away for an age again, will you?"

Nash smiled. "I will be on my best behavior, I promise."

"Good. I need to show you my new collection of thimbles. Papa just brought back the most beautiful one from Scotland. It has a thistle on it."

"You can show them all off very soon." But first he needed to face down his father. "Where is everyone else?"

"Mama and Nelly are visiting. I'm not allowed to go because I fidget too much."

"That's not a bad thing, Hettie. You would find it incredibly dull, I'm sure."

She grinned. "I do not care now that you are here. They shall be jealous I was the first to see you." His sister pouted. "We all missed you terribly."

"I missed you too." He glanced at the study window. "Is Father expecting me?"

"Uh huh. He said for you to go to his study."

Nash gave Hettie another quick embrace. "Go and get your thimbles out. I shall come and see them shortly."

He hoped. That was, if his father didn't send him on his way again.

Straightening his spine, he headed indoors. After handing his jacket, hat, and gloves over to the butler, he traipsed down the corridor toward the study. It all looked the same with the same pictures, the same carpet, the same ink splot that he'd been in huge trouble for when he was seven. But he had changed, and if his father could not see that, then there was nothing that could be done about it.

He knocked on the closed door and waited for permission to enter. Easing open the door, his father rose from his chair. The years had spread the gray from his temples to almost all his thick hair and his shoulders were a little more rounded than Nash remembered. His expression remained guarded but for a moment.

Before Nash could shut the door, his father moved around the desk and threw his arms around Nash.

Nash stilled, his arms frozen at his side. "Uh..."

"My boy." His father stepped back and rubbed a hand over his face. "Forgive me, but we've missed you."

Nash blinked several times. "I, um, missed you too."

His father blew out a breath. "There were too many times that I wanted to come to you but, well, after the way we left things..."

Nash nodded. "I was too proud to come to you."

He clasped Nash's arms and looked him up and down. "You look well, though."

"I am well." If one did not count utterly heartbroken over a woman.

"Good, good. Your mother shall be mightily happy to see you."

"Forgive me, Father, but...well, I really did not think I would be welcome."

"I know." His father grimaced. "And for a while you would not have been. You have to understand how hard it was for me to make that decision but, my boy, you were so lost, and I could not see how else to make you see sense. It seemed the only way to teach you was to hit you where it truly hurt."

Nash nodded. It had hurt. The money and the loss of his family, the loss of his dreams. It had been agonizing, but Nash could see his past self as his father had now. He couldn't be certain he wouldn't do the same thing if he had a son behaving similarly.

"I always thought you would return to us eventually," his father admitted.

"I thought I would not be welcome."

His father pursed his lips. "Why did you think that had changed?"

He shrugged. "I didn't know if it had but I had to try." He gave a slight smile. "I'm different now. I certainly do not gamble, but I...well, I met a woman and she taught me a lot."

"Ah." His gray brows rose. "Women do seem to have that sort of impact on us lowly men. Is this woman still in your life?"

"Not at present, no."

"And there is nothing you can do about that?"

"I do not think so." Grace had been firm in her farewell. She needed time by herself, she said. Then she'd kissed him on the cheek and thanked him for everything. That had seemed fairly final to him.

"Well, if things change, I am certain we would like to meet her." His father clapped a hand to his shoulder. "You do seem rather a new man."

He felt like one in many ways, but was that enough for Grace? He suspected he might just have to summon his courage once more and find out.

Chapter Thirty

Grace tapped her fingers on the breakfast room table and eyed her notes. At the head of the table, her uncle sat, his posture rigid but remaining quiet. He had barely uttered two words to her since they returned home.

She smiled to herself. She knew he was ashamed of his cowardice and maybe a little ashamed of trying to force her to marry Worthington. Even if he wasn't, it didn't matter. She and Aunt Elsie would be moving out as soon as she found a suitable home for them.

Then, she just had to decide what to do about Nash. She had told him she needed time and that was no lie. They had been swept up in some strange event, confined together, and forced into situations that were entirely strange. When he had talked of marrying her to her uncle, for a brief moment, she'd been elated, but she realized that if she were to marry anyone, she could not have it happen in such a way.

She glanced at her notes again. She had hoped that taking the time to just be her own master and, quite frankly, be away from the powerful pull between Nash and her would help her understand things a little bit better.

But it seemed there was nothing to understand. She loved him and no amount of notetaking would help her make sense of such an emotion. She ticked off the list. Nash was kind, loyal, brave, and loving. She also knew he cared for her. He had looked mightily disappointed when she bid him farewell.

But did he love her?

Nothing in her notes could tell her that for certain. She glanced at her aunt, who appeared younger and more relaxed than ever now that their future was settled. Or almost settled. There were plenty of cottages in England to let but Grace kept finding something wrong with them. The bedrooms were too small, or the drawing room didn't get enough sun. There wasn't enough garden for Claude to explore or the proportions of the rooms were not right. She had spent so long dreaming of that future but now it seemed bleak.

Without Nash in it.

The doorbell rang and she glanced up from her scribbles. The door clattered open. "I say there..." said the butler before his words were cut off by something.

Frowning, Grace eyed the entrance to the breakfast room. A little squeak escaped her when a masked man swept into the room, a black scarf covering the bottom half of his face. He pointed a black-gloved finger at her. "Miss Grace Beaumont, I am here to kidnap you."

Her uncle rose to his feet. "What the devil are you playing at?"

Grace blinked a few times, moved her attention from the end of the fingertip, to where a green gaze met her own. She shook her head and smiled. "What are you doing here?"

The corners of Nash's eyes crinkled. "I told you, I am here to kidnap you."

"I am really quite tired of all this kidnapping business." Uncle Charlie sank down onto his chair. "Do what you will with her. I certainly cannot tell her what to do."

Aunt Elsie's mouth hadn't shut since Nash entered the room. She looked between Grace and their intruder. "What is going on, Grace?"

"Oh yes, I forgot." He gestured to Aunt Elsie. "I'm kidnapping you too."

Aunt Elsie put a hand to her chest. "Why would you want to kidnap me?"

"Grace loves you more than anything. I cannot very well have you two apart."

Grace shook her head and smiled. "He is not wrong."

"Good." He gestured for them to both rise. "Consider yourselves kidnapped. Come on, ladies, we do not have all day."

"But...but where are we going?" Aunt Elsie spluttered and looked to Grace. "Do you really want to go with him?"

Grace rose from her chair and looked into Nash's gaze for a moment. She didn't need to think or dwell or hesitate.

"Yes, yes, I do."

"Goodness me, well, I suppose I had better come with you then." Her aunt rose slowly from the chair.

Uncle Charlie poured himself a coffee and withdrew a hipflask from his jacket pocket, adding a healthy dose. "I do not understand what is wrong with women," he muttered. "I really do not."

"Come then, we do not have a moment to lose." Nash took Grace's hand and led her out into the hallway.

"Wait!" She tugged him to a halt. "We cannot go without Claude."

Nash paused. "Of course we cannot. Where is he?"

Grace dashed into her aunt's parlor room and found him curled up on the armchair. He made a little sound of protest when she scooped him up. "Sorry, Claude, but we are going on another adventure."

Outside, a carriage awaited, the livery indicating it belonged to a nobleman. She eyed the crest and glanced back at Nash. "This isn't the crest of a kidnapper."

"It is my father's," he explained. "We have come to an understanding."

"Does that mean you are no longer cut off?"

"It does." He aided Aunt Elsie into the carriage and took Claude from her to hand to her aunt. "And it means you can be assured I do not wish to marry you for money."

She shook her head. "I would never think such a thing of you." She paused. "Marry?"

"Did you really think I was going to take you away and not marry you?"

"If I am honest, you hardly gave me any time to think at all."

"I have a marriage license prepared. All you need to do is say yes and we can be wed and off to Guildham. It's a little worse for wear but I promise I will make it a beautiful home for you and your aunt."

"I do not doubt that."

"Marry?" echoed Aunt Elsie's voice from inside the carriage. "Grace, this doesn't sound very logical."

Grace reached up to undo the black cloth from around Nash's face and flung it to the floor, then put her arms around his neck. "None of this is logical," she murmured. "That's how I know it is right."

"I tried to give you as much time as I could," Nash admitted. "I wanted to give you more but being apart from you was driving me out of my wits. I just knew I had to see you again to be certain."

"There were certainly less dramatic ways you could have done that."

He lifted a shoulder. "Where's the fun in that?"

"I did need that time to myself," she said. "It was good for me, I think. And it made me realize just how much I love you, and I would happily put my fate in your hands."

His smile widened and he looped his arms around her waist. "Did you write notes about me whilst we were apart?"

"Of course."

"Did they say how much I love you?"

She shook her head, the warmth in his gaze stealing any sensible, rational response.

"It's true. I love you, Grace. You and your ugly cat."

"Shh, he thinks he's beautiful."

"*You* are beautiful. In every way possible." He blew out a breath. "Miss Grace Beaumont, you make it impossible to sleep or eat or exist without my thoughts turning to you. Since the moment you thrust that hideous cat at me, I have been obsessed, and I cannot wait to make you my wife."

"Then do not!"

He leaned in and kissed her hard then scooped her up in his arms to carry her into the carriage.

Aunt Elsie shook her head as Grace scooted onto the seat next to her. "It is not like you to do anything so bold."

"No, it is not." She smiled and laced her fingers in her lap. "But I'm different now."

THE END

OTHER TITLES BY SAMANTHA HOLT

MARRIED TO THE RAKE

MARRIED TO THE LORD

MARRIED TO THE EARL

YOU'RE THE ROGUE THAT I WANT

WHEN A ROGUE LOVES A WOMAN

WAITING FOR A ROGUE LIKE YOU

WHAT'S A ROGUE GOT TO DO WITH IT

www.samanthaholtromance.com

Printed in Great Britain
by Amazon